BETROTHED TO THE DRAGON

A DRAGON LOVERS BOOK

KARA LOCKHARTE

SMARTIA
PUBLISHING

Copyright © 2018 by Smartia Publishing

PUBLISHER'S CATALOGING-IN-PUBLICATION DATA

Lockharte, Kara.

Betrothed to the dragon / Kara Lockharte.

San Mateo, CA : Smartia Publishing, 2018. | Dragon Lovers, bk. 1 | Sophie learns that she is betrothed to a dragon who wants her magic, even though she doesn't have any magic of her own.

ISBN 978-1-951431-00-6

Dragons--Fiction. | Paranormal--Fiction. | Magic--Fiction. | Fantasy fiction. | Paranormal romance stories.

LCC PS648.D73 B36 2018 | DDC 813/.54--dc23

Cover design by Jacqueline Sweet

Developmental Editing by Jodi Henley

Copyediting by www.amandajeanedits.com

ALSO BY KARA LOCKHARTE

Kara's Website (with games and interactive stories!)

Kara on Facebook (usually around)

Kara on Instagram (sometimes there)

Kara on Pinterest (once in awhile)

The Space Shifter Chronicles

(Science Fiction Romances)

NOVELS

Wanted by the Werewolf Prince

Taken by the Tigerlord

Desired by the Dragon King (coming soon)

SHORT STORIES

The Boy Who Came Back a Wolf

The Lady and the Tigershifter

In Search of Skye (free to newsletter subscribers)

LICK OF FIRE / Dragon Lovers Series

(Paranormal Romances)

Betrothed to the Dragon

Belonging to the Dragon

Bonded to the Dragon

Abducted by the Angel (coming soon)

Note: This book is a work of fiction. Any resemblance to real life dragonshifter billionaires or anything else else is purely coincidental.

ABOUT BETROTHED TO THE DRAGON

BETROTHED TO THE DRAGON is the FIRST in Kara Lockharte's DRAGON LOVERS mini-series.

I'm engaged to a stranger, a man -- dragon. If I don't marry him, I'm as good as dead.

I've been hiding all my life.

Unlike the rest of my once powerful family, I have no magic.

The immortal monster that ate them all, still hunts me.

And my grandmother thinks that the only way to save me from the monster is to marry me to another monster: a dragon.

Only this monster is perfection in human form: all rippling golden muscle and more gorgeous than anyone who shifts into a scaled monstrous beast has a right to be. His magic calls me, his heat enthralls me and my mind melts at the touch of his inhumanely hot hands on my skin.

There is no way I can marry him.

I know what he truly wants: access to my family's power.

But I have no magic, no power of my own.

He thinks he knows what he's getting with me.

I don't play those games.

It's better to run from a monster, than to marry one.

I'm no dragon's treasure.

Even if my heart wishes otherwise.

Note: This book is a work of fiction. Any resemblance to real life dragon shifter billionaires, or anything else is purely coincidental.

1

———

"WHAT DO YOU MEAN I'M BETROTHED IN AN ARRANGED marriage?"

I glanced at my phone. Only one of the connection bars was filled, indicating barely audible service. I must have heard her wrong. No way my Alexander McQueen-clutch-carrying-Bitcoin-gambling grandmother would say something like that.

"Grandma?"

I checked my phone again and saw the call was disconnected.

Of course. I teetered on the stupid heels I had bought for today, in the museum where I worked. The early twentieth century building was gorgeous with its hand-carved window frames and Italian marble floors but sorely lacking when it came to areas with good mobile service. I danced around a pile of dusty books resting on the floor and navigated through the cubicle maze that passed for the doctoral student office.

Grandma loved playing games. Once, she had played politics with the fate of empires, and now, she invested that talent into stocks and virtual currency.

Outside, I made my way down the great expanse of stone

steps. Fat gray pigeons glared at me, dodging my footsteps. I hit redial on my phone, and she picked up almost immediately. "You lost a bet, right? You know, I'm pretty sure it's not legal to put up your granddaughter's hand in marriage as collateral."

Next to me, Chinese tourists were having a heated discussion about the best pizza places in the Lower East Side.

Grandma exhaled. "No, Sophie. I made the deal so that we would be allowed to come to this country. It was a different, more desperate time."

I had tried to assimilate and adapt to human life in America, with blue jeans, chicken nuggets, and a PhD in Museum Conservation. All of it was easier than remembering what I truly was—the reason why so many of my family members had died.

I paced, trying to release the nervous energy of an all-too-familiar frustration. "I wasn't even a year old. There's no way that will hold up in court."

Grandma made that harrumphing, barking cough she always did when she was done listening to me whine. "Not legal by human standards, no. But by that of our people, yes. I've tried to let you live a life of freedom and make your own choices as much as you could. But my protection won't hold forever. I need to know you are safe. And marriage into this family will protect you." Her voice hardened. "Sophie, you are the last of our line. Even if your power hasn't manifested, the potential of your blood is still there. This is the only way to keep you safe."

I was a black belt in Krav Maga and had extensive firearms training from a grizzled, old ex-Army Ranger sniper who said I had potential, yet none of it mattered. I had to be protected. Unlike my grandmother, my mother, and my father before me, I had no magic.

I stopped pacing and pinched the bridge of my nose. As much as we pretended to be human, we were not.

I clenched the phone tighter. "Why didn't you ever tell me this before?"

"I'd hoped some of the plans I made, the champions I sent against the monster, would succeed before it would come to this." There was a note of sadness in her voice. "But each time it fights, it learns. And every day, it grows more and more powerful."

My alarm vibrated, startling me into dropping my phone. I tried to catch it, but it was too late. When I picked it up, there was a hairline crack on the screen. Wonderful.

I picked up the phone, turned on the speaker, and spoke louder than I intended, so much so that it startled the pigeons around me into grudging hops. "Grandma, I have to get ready for my talk."

"There is more that I have to tell you. But we'll talk more later. Good luck on your presentation, Sophie." She hung up because she knew I was in no mood to say goodbye.

More? What more could she tell me? Next, she'd be revealing I was actually a human adoptee. That would have been less of a surprise.

The picture of us appeared on my phone's lock screen.

We looked so different, she and I. Grandma, with her white skin and straight hair, and me with my dark skin and wavy semi-curls. The only thing we shared was our eye-shape that humans called Asian. In school, I had always checked off whatever box felt more convenient at the time. African, Asian, Caucasian, Hispanic—I had convincingly claimed them all. Grandma scoffed at the idea of labeling ourselves according to human ideas of ethnicity.

"Our family spans the Earth," she had said. "A shen does not identify herself by the tribal groupings of humans any more than a lion distinguishes itself by the particulars of ant kingdoms." As much as we looked like and pretended to be, we weren't human. We were the first intelligent life forms on this planet and are connected to the deep magical nodes of the Earth. Humans had many names for us: fae, yokai, djinn, apsaras, gods, demons, monsters and so on, never realizing we were all one people. It was strange that humans hadn't, considering what a wide range of colors, shapes, and abilities humans themselves came in. Genghis Khan, Gandhi and Gertrude Stein had all been human, but were as different from one another as water was from fire. And yet, somehow, humans made the assumption that physical appearance for magical shape-shifting creatures meant we were all different species.

We weren't. We may have had different strengths, different magics, but from gorgons to thunderbirds to naga, we were all just shen.

But years and years of intermingling with humans had dissipated most of our legendary magic.

And for the remaining shen with magic? None of it was enough to fight the Devourer when it had entered this world, seeking new victims.

Including my parents.

They had died to save me, not knowing how they had thrown their lives away for the unforgivably flawed shen I was.

My phone buzzed again with the alarm I'd set to prepare for the one event I'd been dreading and anticipating for the last six months. It was time for my post-dissertation fellowship presentation on religious motifs in East and Near Eastern art at the museum.

———

GIVING the public lecture as required by my fellowship put worms in my stomach so much more than defending the actual dissertation in front of a panel of peers and experts. I had to simplify things, touch upon other areas that weren't necessarily my specialty, and make the topic more appealing to the public; even I could admit that a discussion about the proper application of persimmon juice in scrollwork conservation could get pretty dry.

I swiped at the tablet in my hand, changing the slide display. An image of a Tlingit wood carving of a woman with closed eyes, surrounded by mouths and dripping with blood, was paired side by side with that of a Heian Japanese scroll painting.

"And as you can see, the image of the Devourer is one found across several cultures, from ancient Rome to Heian Japan to the totemic carvings of the Tlingit peoples of the First Nations of Canada."

I clicked through the slides, kept moving, kept talking, even as I tried to ignore the striking gaze of the man in the back of the room. He had entered about five minutes into my talk, and I couldn't figure out why I was so aware of him.

It was foolish of me to include the Devourer. But I had felt a strange streak of defiance Grandma once said was the lot of the young and reckless.

And yet, she had, oddly enough, given her blessing for me to speak of the monster.

"Little fox, as difficult as things are, I want you to bloom as you can, not in fear."

He couldn't be working for the Devourer, could he?

Long ago, there had been good reason for people not to call the names of gods or monsters in vain. In a sense, I was doing that here.

I walked across the stage, my heels clicking loudly.

"Of course, it is not the only common motif across cultures. Dragons are another common motif..."

For all my fear and worry, the actual talk went by faster than I expected. As the crowd dissipated, my future boss—the assistant curator of the renowned Metro NYC museum—came up to me. Even in heels, I still found myself looking up at the tall black woman. Her British accent was as crisp as the pleats in her trousers. "That was excellent, Sophie. You handled those questions quite nicely."

The tall, broad-shouldered man dawdled in the back of the room, leaning against the wall, swiping at his phone as the crowd flowed around him. Why was he hanging around? There was something extraordinary about him that I couldn't quite figure out, yet the dark business suit with an open collar and loose tie made him seem like he was just another worker on a lunch break.

"Um, thanks." His suit appeared tailored to him, but I couldn't shake the feeling it was more disguise than truth. No, he wouldn't be just another worker, not with that confidence and stance. More like a CEO.

She followed my line of sight and smiled. "That one is quite tidy."

He glanced upward, saw us looking, and smiled. The sound in the room fell away for a single heartbeat and filled my ears with a slow, loud thump.

I blinked.

Everything returned to normal. Except he was...closer? Walking over to me?

My boss winked. "Oh, to be young again. He must have a question."

"Oh um, I uh—"

I blinked. "What?"

"Answer his questions. It's part of the requirement that you answer questions from the public, after all." She winked. "I'll see you later."

My heart sped up as he approached.

"Hi." My voice came out higher than I'd intended, and I looked up at him. "Did you have any questions about the talk?"

He looked at me with golden light-brown eyes. He had runway-model cheekbones and the kind of chin that jutted from the bands of Roman centurion helmets.

I had the strangest feeling that his gaze was stripping me, not just of my clothes but to some invisible core. My muscles unreasonably tensed, ready to fight or flee; maybe both at the same time.

His smooth bass voice rolled across my skin like a caress. "I have many questions, none of which I have time to ask."

"Well, umm, there's going to be another talk in, umm—" I glanced at my watch, even though I knew precisely when the next talk would be. "About an hour?" Dammit, why had I made that sound like a question?

The corner of those full lips quirked up into a smile. "Will you be leading it?"

"No."

"A shame." He turned, looked over his shoulder, and nodded at me. "I enjoyed listening to you."

2

PERHAPS IT WAS THE NEWS ABOUT MY SUPPOSED BETROTHAL, OR maybe it was just relief my talk was over, but afterward, I felt restless, as if electricity lurked under my skin.

And I couldn't stop thinking about the way that man had looked at me, like...he saw me.

Shen have control over the physical appearance of their descendants' human form, and Grandma had designed mine to be perfectly ordinary. Wavy dark-brown hair, brown skin in the perfect blend of my mother and father's coloring in human form, and brown eyes hidden behind glasses. When Grandma had realized I would have no shen abilities, she made sure to give enough proportionality to my features that with some clever makeup and clothing, I could gain attention, should I wish it.

And he had looked at me like he could see through it all.

I shook my head in a futile effort to shake out the image. New York City had more than nine million people in it: the chances I would see him again were immensely small.

Besides, I had more important things to worry about, like the fact that Grandma's magical protection was weakening.

My shoulder tingled in the spot where Grandma had placed her hand and traced the sigil of protection on me so long ago. It still held.

For now, I still had my freedom.

I leaned back in my squeaking chair, my feet finally free of the stupid heels. I was alone in the doctoral student office. Late-afternoon sun streamed through the window in bars of light so sharp, they were almost solid, save for the dancing dust motes. At this time of year, there would be plenty of light to run and plenty of people running as well.

Safety was to be found in the human herd.

I grabbed the bag underneath my desk, changed in the bathroom, and in minutes, I was out under the trees, running, running, running.

I ran as fast as I could, escaping the thoughts that troubled me. I focused on the charging beats pounding in my headphones, yet Grandma's words kept coming back to me.

Betrothed.

Arranged.

Marriage.

My heart pounded, blood thumped, and my breath quickened, but my mind held on to those words like a woman grasping a pole for balance in a crowded subway.

I turned the corner and headed down an empty stretch.

A long time ago, Grandma had advised closing my eyes and letting out mental screams. It was a good way to relieve stress, release emotions, and, of course, to temporarily disorient any nearby mind readers.

For just a moment, I closed my eyes and screamed in my mind, the way my grandmother had taught me.

I slammed into a wall. Pain exploded through my body. I found myself sprawled on my ass, hard bits of gravel digging in and cutting skin.

"Are you okay?" a familiar resonant male voice asked.

I looked up and found black running shorts against a defined set of abs, flanked by rippling striated muscle up to a wall of pecs. His sunglasses were askew, and his tawny golden eyes gazed at me with an indescribable expression.

Immediately, my cheeks flooded even warmer. I knew exactly who he was—the man from the museum—and my breath hitched in my throat, as I couldn't think of a thing to say.

He repeated his question, offering me his hand. "Are you okay?"

I squeezed my eyes shut in embarrassment. Let's just pretend I hadn't just made a giant fool of myself. "I'm sorry. I didn't see you."

He knelt and looked me over. His scent of salt and man and something else unexpectedly alluring was surprising. "You don't look injured."

He picked up something beside me and slowly handed it to me. "Unfortunately, I can't say the same about your phone."

I stared at my shattered phone. I tried to turn it on. There was a bright flare, and then, it died.

"Be careful," he said. "Broken edges can be sharp."

I let out a low groan. "I didn't even know phones could break like this. I just downloaded a digital subway pass."

"Let me guess, without the subway app on your phone, you're stuck," he said.

Another jogger ran by, and belatedly, I realized I was still on the ground. I shifted to get up, and he offered his hand again. Without a thought, I took it and found his big, warm hand closing around mine, pulling me up effortlessly.

"Listen," he said. "I'm sorry about your phone. It was my fault it broke. Let me write you a check for it. I don't live far from here. If you need to, you can use my phone to call someone."

"Thanks. But I'll be fine," I said, the words automatic and

tumbling out of my mouth before I could stop myself. I didn't like accepting help from strangers. Especially handsome ones.

He looked at me with his unfiltered golden gaze that held an impossible temptation I knew I couldn't indulge in now. Fuck, why couldn't I have met him yesterday?

"Let me make it up to you." He was hot, beautiful, and he stared at me like I was too.

The invisible sigil on my shoulder tingled, reminding me of my grandmother, the secret betrothal, the determination of my future without so much as a what-do-you-think-Sophie. Just because I didn't have magic didn't mean I shouldn't have a say in who was going to be my husband.

Arranged marriage, my ass.

"Actually, I might take you up on that offer." I wiped my hand on my shorts and offered it to him. "I'm Sophie."

He looked at my hand for a moment before taking it. "Hunter," he said, almost expectantly.

"Are you on TV or something?"

He laughed and squeezed my hand. Strangely enough, I had the oddest sense I had just been caught.

———

I HAD NEVER BEEN slow by any means. In high school, I had run track and kept up with my running as much as I could.

After all, running was a skill that might save my life one day.

And as much as I knew I was fast, I had the distinct sense that, despite Hunter's size and bulk, he could easily catch me if he wanted to. His strides were long, and he moved with an easy quickness.

He ran with me to the museum and waited for me outside while I darted into the office and grabbed my bag. We walked the remainder of the way to his place, and true to his word, he did live close by. In fact, he lived in the very building I admired every day on my way to work. With ornately carved 1920s art deco eagles, their wings widespread, it was a favorite location for movie shoots, and tourists often lingered in front of it.

He pointed toward the arched courtyard entrance, which very few buildings in Manhattan had.

I forced myself not to gawk or stutter in amazement. "Convenient."

"It is," he replied, nodding to the turbaned Sikh doorman who addressed him as "Mr. Hunter."

"Mr. Hunter?" I followed Hunter's lead back toward a set of elevator doors. They opened. Hunter gestured for me to enter before him, so I did. Something about his presence behind me made me automatically press myself against the back wall to make room for him.

"That's how they do things in this building." He stood next to me—so close, we were almost touching.

In the tiny space, I was surrounded by more of that strangely delicious scent of his. I trained my eyes ahead, determined not to stare at the fine sheen of sweat that clung to his biceps, which were easily the size of my head.

He inserted a brass metal key in the slot, turned it, and hit the PH button. Of course, he would be in the penthouse. Where else would he be?

Apartments in buildings like this were treasures to be held on to for generations. "Has your family lived in this building for long?"

"Not exactly. It was won in a game of chance."

"High stakes."

His pirate's smile spoke of gambling treasures at the flick of a wrist. "No fun playing if it's not."

The elevator chimed, and the doors opened into a tastefully

modern and crisp living room decorated mostly in neutral shades of gray and white with a dash of color here and there.

A song lyric popped into my head: *Into the dragon's lair walked the maiden.*

He strolled in. "Relax. I'll get you my phone and some water."

I walked in slowly across the threshold, following him past the living room toward the remodeled open-kitchen area. It was all silver and gray, as empty and pristine as a magazine spread, save for the phone plugged almost carelessly into an outlet above a counter.

I took a seat at the island counter. "You don't spend a lot of time here, do you?"

"Is it that obvious? I travel a lot for work." He unplugged the phone, tapped at it, and set it before me. "I opened my banking app. Just type your email and whatever you think a new phone costs and send it off."

"You're very trusting," I said, teasing him. "How do you know I'm not going take all your money?"

Hunter looked me over with that penetrating gaze of his. "I don't," he said. It felt almost like a test. Abruptly, he turned his back on me. "The pin is 3752 in case it goes to sleep. I'm going to rinse off and put on some clean clothes."

I tried not to think of him naked in the shower, but the mental image brought a warmth to my skin that was hard to ignore.

I picked up his phone and swiped the banking app away. The lock screen appeared, which showed a yellowed image of another man with Hunter's chin and a woman with his eyes, laughing in a candid shot. It was a digital photo of a physical photograph. I knew from experience that people our age didn't normally carry around photographs of parents in their youth.

Not unless there was tragedy involved.

I had photos of my parents as wallpaper on my phone as well.

I crossed my legs and typed in the pin. The wallpaper image was replaced by another, this one of palm trees and a white sand beach.

I stared dumbly at the phone. Who would I call? My roommate was off in Asia somewhere, and my grandmother wasn't even in the city. The easiest thing to do would be to just borrow some subway fare, which irked me. If family stories had taught me anything, it was to never place myself in debt to a human.

Not that he would ever know I was anything other than what I seemed.

I held his phone, trying hard to resist the urge to snoop. Photos? Emails? Contacts? His entire life was in my hands.

I stared at the image of palm trees. Wait, wasn't that like a default image? Warily, I swiped through. No apps other than the standard. As devoid of personality as his apartment, save for the lock screen.

How strange.

He came back with wet hair, wearing a button-down shirt with sleeves tight across his biceps.

He smelled of the most generic soap and shampoo, yet it was totally distracting. I set his phone down quickly. Even though he had handed it to me, for some reason, I suddenly felt like I wasn't supposed to be holding it in the first place.

I rested my elbow on the counter and perched my chin in the palm of my hand. "What is it that you do again?"

He set a glass of water in front of me. An ice cube clinked against the glass. "A little bit of this, a little bit of that."

I ran my finger around the rim of the glass, ignoring the phone. Time to start calling him on his mysterious-handsome-stranger act. "That is the most informative non-response ever."

His lips quirked up in a smile. He leaned toward me, laying

his thick forearms across the counter. "Interested in my whole life story, then? Where should I start?"

I matched his movement and leaned in closer. "You really going to tell me?"

"Well, I can start with my first memory: holding on to a stuffed pink elephant named Fanfan." The thought of this serious, rugged man clinging to a stuffed pink elephant made me burst into laughter. His face cracked into a smile that irritatingly, made my heart beat faster. My life was complicated enough without meeting a man whose smile would have sirens singing.

"Did you reach anyone?"

"Nope. Don't know anyone's number. It was all in my phone. Can I borrow some subway fare?"

He took a sip of water from his glass and then looked inside it. Apparently, the ice within was fascinating. "You know, if you need a ride home, I could take you."

I picked up my glass and examined my ice just as intently. "You'll rescind that offer once I tell you where I live."

He grimaced. "You live in Jersey, don't you? Let me guess —Hoboken."

I put the phone down. "Now, that's almost insulting."

"Hey, some of my closest friends are from Hoboken. Nothing wrong with being from Jersey."

I looked at him, and we both burst into laughter again at the same time.

"Queens," I said.

"Well, at least it's not Hoboken," he said.

We laughed again.

"I'm serious. The car is downstairs, and when the traffic lightens up in an hour or two, I'll take you home."

An hour or two with him. The prospect was tantalizing. With a man this handsome, it was too good to be true. It wasn't that I suffered from a lack of self-confidence; it was more that I was pragmatically aware of how ordinary and unforgettable I looked, especially compared to the head-turning beauty of my mother and grandma in their prime. For me, in this day and age, beauty was a weapon that could be used to find me.

Yet, he looked at me with those golden eyes like I was the most captivating woman in the world.

Perhaps he was one of those humans who could sense magic. Some humans were drawn to it, even if they didn't know what it was. And despite evidence to the contrary, Grandma said there was magic in my blood, even if I couldn't use it or manipulate it.

This was why I preferred being around humans. They didn't look at me with pity in their eyes.

I imagined myself to be Grandma, one of the greatest magic wielders of the shen, always confident and never self-conscious. "If I do take you up on that offer, Hunter," I said, making my voice linger over his name, "what would you suggest we do for one or two hours?"

The air condition clicked on, and a hum filled the room. Cold air blasted me from above. My nipples tightened from the temperature change, and his eyes flicked to my chest.

His pupils dilated. Heat simmered within me at his response, low beneath my belly. "I can think of a few things," he said.

I couldn't help but swallow. What was I thinking? I wasn't my Grandma; I had no experience playing this game. I didn't do the one-night-stand thing with a man I'd just met. Maybe it was the shen in me, but I liked getting to know someone—the chase, the interplay, the hunt. Even if I wasn't much of a shen when it came to magic, we had all once been hunters.

I crossed my arms and shifted to the next stool over, away from the air conditioning. "In the museum," I said carefully, enunciating the words to show that I wasn't brain-fogged by him. "You said you had questions for me. Here's your chance."

Hunter laughed. He came around the counter to take a seat on the stool next to me. He swiveled the stool toward me, and he was so big, his knees almost touched mine. "Open season on Sophie for questions. I like it."

I gave him my fakest sultry look. "Anything you want to know about universal motifs in ancient Near Eastern and East Asian religious artifacts, I'm your girl."

His grin was full blown but was as far from his eyes as a desert from the ocean. "I want to know more about the woman with the mouths."

3

I LOOKED AT THE GLASS IN MY HAND, SWIRLED THE WATER AROUND, and listened to the ice clink as I unsuccessfully tried to repress the chill of the room. Of all things, he would choose to ask about the menace. The monster that had killed my family over the centuries and hunted us until there were almost none left.

I swallowed, forced brightness into my voice. "Yes?"

"What do you think she represents?"

"The Chinese, Mayans, and Greeks have similar names for her. Devourer. Eater. Mother of Teeth." I kept my voice as neutral as possible while inside, my instincts were screaming to change the subject as quickly as possible. "But they are all clear on what she is. Death."

"Are there any stories of the Devourer being defeated?"

It was why I had started studying the Devourer in the first place. I wanted to know if the monster had ever been beaten.

"The Devourer is death," I said, remembering a line from an Akkadian poem. "And Death cannot be defeated."

His question had hit too close today. I didn't want to think about it anymore.

"Your phone," I said. "Are those two people your parents?"

He looked away, his long fingers curving around the water glass. "Yes."

The ensuing silence was a terrible sort of affirmation. I reached out to cover his hand. He looked at me, and there was a blankness in his gaze I recognized all too well.

"I never knew mine. I was raised by my grandmother."

He let go of the glass and entwined our fingers. His hands were big and incongruously rough.

"Sometimes it's better, I think, that I didn't know them," I said. "Because to know that love and lose it..." I had become familiar with the kind of pity reflected in his eyes. But from him, it wasn't as irritating, maybe because he too had been shaped by a similar loss.

His hand closed tighter on mine as his voice bent to a more serious tone. "I treasure every memory I have of my parents. As few as they are." We looked at each other, in this moment of understanding. He slowly stroked the back of my hand with his thumb.

I struggled to think of a something coherent and relevant to say. I settled on something about childhood. "When I was younger, I would sometimes feel guilty for missing them because I loved my grandmother, and part of me felt like I was being ungrateful." I wasn't even sure if he knew he was touching me, but his thumb mesmerized me. "Especially every Mother's and Father's Day at school when we were forced to make craft gifts to bring home."

His thumb stopped as he replied, "I once brought home a card with a tie. We had just come to this country, and my grandmother thought it was a noose."

I let out a laugh and reveled in his responding smile.

Wait a minute, we were still holding hands.

"I have to admit," he said, "you are not what I expected."

My pulse sped up. "Oh, what did you expect?"

There was a confident, knowing gleam in his eye. Hunter knew the effect of his words on me. "I don't know. I like you a lot more than I thought I would."

His words buoyed and punched me at the same time. "I like you too, Hunter." I knew I should tell him about my betrothal, even if I wasn't going through with it.

He leaned in, his face above mine.

"May I kiss you?" he asked as though he were as proper as a lord in Victorian England.

I knew I had to tell him. I swear I was going to.

"Yes."

The moment his lips were on mine, I forgot my objections, forgot the betrothal, and forgot the monster hunting me. All I could think about was Hunter, kissing me. I slid off my stool and moved into the intimate space between his open legs. My hands were on his waist, and through the thin white cloth, I could feel the muscular indentations of the V of his hips. His fingers skimmed the hem of my shirt, leaving hot trails on my skin.

I was already so close to being mostly naked with just a T-shirt, a sports bra, and skin-clinging running shorts. I should stop. I wasn't being cautious. He was a stranger. There was a betrothal...because of all those reasons and more.

But his touch was mesmerizing, his mouth even more so, coaxing, beckoning. Heat bloomed within me. I gave in to a reck-less urge and fumbled at the buttons of his shirt. I loved the way he startled at my fingertips on his bare skin. He pressed harder against me.

I turned my head, breaking away from his kiss. "I don't usually do this," I said.

"Neither do I," he replied, a hot whisper licking my ear. His hands slid up my shirt. Never had I been so thankful for my obsession in finding sports bras with actual back clasps as he undid my bra.

He pulled back and pinned me with that golden gaze. "This is the time to tell me to stop, Sophie." There was something feral and not quite human in the way he looked at me. I didn't know who he was, didn't know what game was being played, and, at this moment, didn't care. No one had ever made me feel this way before, so hot, so wanton that I would burst into flames if I didn't have him now.

And it might possibly be my last chance to make a choice like this, one that was wholly mine.

I reached for him and tugged his shirt upward. "If you stop, Hunter, I will hunt you down."

He stopped with an almost comical look of disbelief at my terrible pun. It made him seem more human, and, ironically, made me want him even more.

I burst into nervous laughter.

He grinned, his hands on my hips. "You're going to pay for that."

He lifted me, eliciting a yelp of surprise, and set me on the bar. Now, I was the one who spread open my legs as he closed the distance between us. The stone of the countertop was cold against my ass, a delicious contrast to the inferno at my core.

His mouth was on my ear, and he pressed his hard, male body against me. "I'm going to taste you. Here," he said, placing a finger on my lips. I licked him and was gratified by a squeeze of my ass, pulling me closer. "Here," he said, cupping my breast. He slid his hand downward, past the elastic waistband, up into the leg of my shorts. "Most especially here," he said, stroking the damp crotch of my panties. Hot, delicious need surged with his words, with his touch, burning away my common sense. I had just met him; he was a stranger, yet the knowledge, the reckless danger, only made me want to fuck him more.

"And just when you think you can't take anymore, I'm going to fuck you so well, you'll masturbate to the memory for the rest of your life." He slid a finger into my panties, stroking that sensitive bud with his thumb. I gasped at the desire in my veins. "Are my intentions clear?"

"Promises, promises," I said, as he slipped a finger inside me.

My sex clenched around him, and he smiled. "Just the truth," he said.

Truth.

He slipped another finger inside me, and I shuddered.

I gripped his shoulders. I'd never understood the expression "dazed with desire" until now. I felt drunk, wanton, and if he didn't fuck me soon, I would die.

"Hunter." I put my hand up. I pushed him back, but it was like pushing a wall. "Wait." When he realized what I was doing, he withdrew and eased up.

It was bizarre, but the absence of his touch made me feel cold.

My words, came tumbling out in a rush, escaping my attempts to be cool and calm. "I have to be honest. It doesn't really matter, but I want you to know that I'm betrothed."

He stopped and looked at me like I had just smacked him in the head with a bat. "Betrothed," he repeated.

My chances with him were evaporating. I said as quickly as I could, "To a man I've never met, in an agreement I never made."

He raked his hand through his thick hair, taking a step back. "What?"

I was losing him. A bizarre, terrifying desperation gripped me, one that was wildly out of proportion to how long I had known him. "My grandmother arranged it on my behalf when I was a child. I didn't even know about it until today."

He blinked and stared at me as if he didn't recognize me. "Today," he repeated.

"Just before I gave my talk at the museum." I forced a weak laugh. "She has the worst timing."

"You didn't know?" he asked, almost biting out the words.

Shit. He was really pissed. I wasn't sure if that was a good thing or not.

I slid off the counter, my heart pounding and stomach sinking. Better to have this conversation now, I knew, but still, this sucked. The realization sunk into my limbs like weights. "I refuse to believe that I'm beholden to any promise made on my behalf, without my knowledge. I am not chattel to be bartered."

"So, you intend to break the betrothal?" he asked.

I rehooked by bra and folded my arms across my chest. According to Grandma, it was the only way I would be safe from the monster. "I don't know."

He looked at me, his gaze so intense, I had to take a step back. I was trying to think of what to say, but he spoke first. "You should have a say in who you choose to marry," he said finally. He turned. "Wait here. There's something I want to show you."

The air conditioning clicked on again, making the room seem colder without his presence. Whatever had been about to happen between us wasn't going to happen now. Disappointment mixed with sexual frustration made me want to punch something.

There was a vibrating noise. A message flashed itself with a disturbingly familiar image.

I generally didn't go around reading other people's messages, ever.

But this...

I entered the PIN he had told me and read the message displayed.

Cold dread seeped through my veins at the information.

"Sophie?" Hunter's questioning voice came from behind me.

He stopped when he saw the look on my face and me with his phone.

I put on my calm war face, the one my grandmother had made me practice, even though my heart was racing.

I held up the screen so he could see it. "'Here is the rest of the information on your betrothed; apologies if some of this is in duplicate: Sophie May,'" I said, starting with the first message. "'Daughter of Yi-Fan and Breaker-of-Storms. Grandmother, Lady Keiko Asakusa. PhD Candidate in Art History. Assistant Curator at the New York Metropolis Museum of Art.'"

I swiped to the next one. "'Required wedding date—'"

His big hand was suddenly wrapped around my wrist. "It's not what it looks like."

At that moment, if I'd had magic, I would have burned him to a crisp. I had been on the verge of having sex with him, and...

And...

I couldn't think about it, I was so angry. If I had been a true shen, there would be things exploding around me and lights flickering. Instead, I was limited to what I could convey with my voice. "Let. Me. Go."

He released me.

I backed away from him, sidling toward the door. "Why the pretense, my dear *betrothed*?" I put as much disgust into the word as I could.

"Seeing you at the museum, yes, that was intentional. But running into you at the park, that was not." He shook his head. "I thought you knew. I thought you were playing shen games."

That would be a shen thing to do. But I was never good at those sorts of things.

"Shen games," I repeated. The way he said it, implied he wasn't shen. Which didn't make sense. On Earth, there were humans, and there were shen. Shen who had human form but who also had access to deeper magics and other physical forms with horns, tails, wings, scales and many more. I was the strange anomaly of being shen with no magic.

"I am not shen," he said. He held his hand out. A ball of flame appeared in his palm. It flickered in a way that no natural flame did. Smokeless, colorful, and mesmerizing.

No shen could manifest such power in their human form.

Dragon.

My grandmother had betrothed me to a dragon.

I took a step back. "This can't be for real."

Long ago, around the time Rome fell, my father had tried to bar the dragons' arrival to this world, when they'd arrived as refugees from a dying planet. The same monster that had destroyed their world had followed them to Earth.

And instead of hunting them, it had turned its attention to the shen.

"You brought the Devourer to Earth," I said slowly. "You are the reason the shen are nearly gone."

"I was born in New York," he said. "My parents may have been immigrants, but I was born on Earth. We are alike, you and I."

I turned. "No," I said vehemently. "Because I didn't agree to any of this." I began pacing. "Why the hell would Grandma do this?"

"You are a child of Earth. And your bloodline goes back to the very formation of this planet," said Hunter, so, so maddeningly calm.

The potential of your blood is still there.

"This is why the betrothal was arranged," I said, bitterness emerging from my voice. "You're here because you need my bloodline."

His eyes met mine. "Truthfully, when they told me, I wasn't too thrilled either. But I've changed my mind."

Nobody, not even the shen, knew much about the dragons because they were literally aliens to this world. But there were still stories of what dragons did. Sex was often a way to create a permanent magical enslavement bond of sorts. My voice raised in incredulity. "Were you going to 'seal' me with sex?"

His lack of denial was all I needed. "I thought you knew."

Impossible, infuriating heat began welling up within me. He hadn't actually wanted me, just the magic in my blood.

I had almost lost my freedom. He had been planning to *enslave* me. My stomach turned at the thought. I backed away, holding up my hand. "We're done here."

He came forward. "You can't expect to just leave."

I grabbed my bag and headed for the door. "I am leaving. I'm still free to do that."

"You have no ride home."

"I'll walk if I have to." I tried to open the door, but it was locked. There was no knob, which meant it was probably a fingerprint or a phone-controlled lock. I spun on my heel and found him closer than I had expected, but thankfully, not as close as he could have been. "Are you going to keep me here against my will?"

There was a grim look on his face. "Your grandmother's protection won't last forever."

For some reason, it only made me even more pissed.

I tried the door again. Still locked.

I turned back to him, and he tapped at his phone.

"I swear I'm going to break this door down if you don't let me out." Fear, rather than anger, probably would have been a more reasonable emotion at this moment because, after all, he was an actual dragon with all the magic he possessed at his command and I had none. No tricks, no trinkets, nothing. But I was so angry at myself for believing in this delusion that reason seemed like a distant land I'd once known.

The phone beeped, the lock clicked, and the door opened.

"I've called a car service for you," he said.

I marched into the elevator and jammed the door-close button as hard as I could.

The doors slid together much too slowly.

"Take the car, number eighty-eight," he said.

The elevator closed behind me.

4

I WAS DETERMINED NOT TO TAKE HIS FANCY CAR SERVICE.

But on cue, the moment I stepped out, rain unleashed itself in a torrential downpour. Either I took the car service or I drowned on the streets of New York City.

So, I took his goddamned car service.

The fucker.

Images of his mouth on me flashed in my head.

I couldn't believe his gall.

I couldn't believe I had actually let myself think something was possible between us.

He had tried to permanently "seal" me.

It was known dragons could "seal" others into their magical service, creating some sort of magical connection and servitude.

Or so the shen had long believed.

I rubbed my eyes, thinking, trying to remember what, if anything, I knew about dragon sealing bonds. Wait, what had grandma said? Something along the lines of "shen don't know what they don't know. And dragons keep their secrets." I twisted a lock of my hair around my finger, my mind running through the few dragon stories I knew. A few years back, some dragon

29

had thought it funny to pass off their epic stories as a children's book, and at the time, I wasn't sure why Grandma had made me read it.

There was a story about a red balloon and a magic cat with a father saving his son through their seal, which suggested it was some sort of connection.

But only if the story was actually true. And though fairy tales tended to have a core of truth, it was the details that were often inaccurate.

Let me be clear about my intentions.

I thought you were playing shen games.

I balled up my fists. I wasn't going to cry.

The car service dropped me off, and I dashed into my building, keys at the ready, and slogged up the five flights of stairs to the top floor. Dim lights filled the hallway, flickering as they usually did. It wasn't a terrible neighborhood, nor was it a terrible building, but it was old.

I was never so glad as when I undid the triple locks and shoved the door open to the darkened apartment.

And was greeted by an odd, almost burnt-metallic sort of odor.

For a moment, I wondered if Chloe was experimenting with her potions again. That was the problem with having a witch as a roommate. Usually, it was pretty awesome because it meant no roaches or rats would dare cross the boundaries she had set, but sometimes, it meant our apartment smelled like a cross between bacon and old shoes.

Then, I remembered she was still in Seoul.

I dropped my bags. "Hello?" I called, flipping on the light switch. I reached for my grandma's large black umbrella in the stand by the door. She had left it behind on her last visit, saying something about stormy weather coming when you least expected it.

"Is anyone here?"

All seemed normal. A purple throw was slung over the grey couch we'd found on the street. It had taken us an entire day to haul it up here. In front of the couch was a wooden crate that served as a coffee table, the letters KXA stenciled on it in red. There was an empty mug with a tea bag, a few celebrity gossip magazines.

And yet there was that smell.

"Chloe," I pretended to call to my roommate. "Are you here?" It was probably nothing, but I decided to keep up the pretense as I moved slowly into the apartment. "All the guys are waiting downstairs for our double date. You remember, John the cop and his hot brother, Mark the Navy Seal."

No answer.

Her bedroom door was open. My bedroom door was closed.

I never left my bedroom door closed. I didn't like the idea of someone or something jumping out.

I backed away. I was in an enclosed space. No phone. No magic.

But there were things that chased you if you ran and could sometimes be frightened if you confronted them fast.

I took a deep breath, braced myself with the umbrella, stomped over, and kicked open the bedroom door.

Sophie.

I froze. "Grandma?"

In my bedroom, more bed, than actual room, my grandmother sat in a cross-legged position, levitating a foot off the mattress. Her eyes were closed, and a soft glow emanated from her.

"Grandma?"

She opened her eyes, and for a moment, the glow was so blinding, it was like staring into the sun, too bright to be her.

It wasn't my grandmother but a message she had left for me.

"The Devourer is here. I'm going to take it on a run for as long as I can, my darling girl, but I can't hold it off forever."

Hot tears came unbidden to my eyes. "No! Wait—"

"Find your fiancé. I've texted you the information you need to find him. Marry him, and his family will protect you."

"But—"

"Don't 'but' me, young lady. Save yourself, if not for yourself, then for our future."

My grandmother's image faded.

Grandma.

I sank to my knees. There was a vast hole in my chest. Grandma had been preparing me for this moment ever since I could remember.

Do not *look for me.*

But it was like preparing for death or for a truck to hit you: you couldn't really know until it happened. And now, not only had the truck hit, it was a tractor-trailer speeding over my broken heart.

Do not *think you can defeat a monster that has eaten the greatest of the shen.*

I looked at my stupid, magic-less hands.

Run, little fox. All you can do is run.

And it was worse so much worse than I had ever thought it would be.

Heat, anger, and uselessness filled me. I hated what I was, hated that I could not be what my grandmother needed me to be. My mother, my father, and now my grandmother had sacrificed their lives so I could live. And for what?

All for a magical null.

Leaving me no choice but to go beg for magical protection from a man, a dragon, who had tried to enslave me without my knowledge.

I thought you were playing shen games.

Did he really think I had known? Even now, I could feel the lingering of the heated trails he had left on my skin.

You should have a say in who you choose to marry.

He had stopped when I told him I was betrothed.

I thought you knew.

Grandma, I mouthed, voiceless, my throat utterly closed with grief. She was gone. And I was next.

A chill went through me. The monster had destroyed the dragons, had chased them here. How did she expect that Hunter could protect me when it had carved swathes through armies of dragons? Why would the dragons be able to protect me when they hadn't even been able to save themselves?

Or maybe we were all destined to die and this was just an effort to stave off the inescapable end.

Unless Grandma knew something, I didn't.

I laughed, tears streaming from my eyes. To say Grandma had her secrets was like saying a fox had fur.

If I went to Hunter now, would he be honorable and fulfill the bargain that had been made?

I clenched my fists. First, I had to get to him. Details later.

I left a note for Chloe, who was more than capable of taking care of herself. The monster wanted shen blood, and Chloe's human magic was easily disguisable. I packed a bag with basic clothes, a toothbrush, and Grandma's umbrella, along with enough emergency cash and cards to keep me on the run. I headed to the local bodega, bought two phones—the cheap, disposable kind—and realized I didn't even have Hunter's number. I didn't even know his last name. Using the phone, I logged into the cloud to find whatever details Grandma had on Hunter.

Only when I logged in, the screen went black. White letters scrolled across it.

IT'S USELESS TO RUN.

I threw the phone into the street where it was promptly run over by a yellow cab.

The rain had stopped, leaving a humid haze in the air. Deep puddles lay with that shimmering iridescence of motor oil and other city chemicals permeating the streets. I darted around them, heading toward the subway. At least I knew where Hunter lived. I was determined not to marry him, but perhaps I could make some other kind of deal. Dragons were known for their insistence on bargains; on fair, equal exchanges.

"Hey, chicky-chicky," said a white guy leaning against the wall. He looked like the human version of a bulldog, with a crooked nose, spiked collar, and a shaved head.

I avoided eye contact with him as I hurried by.

Suddenly, he hooked my arm and dragged me back.

"I was talking to you, girly-yo. You should pay attention when a man is talking to you."

I slipped out of his grasp easily and faced him. I clutched the umbrella, but kept my elbows in, squared shoulders, and balanced feet ready for quick movement, as I had been trained. "You don't want to be doing this."

He laughed. "Is the little brown girly-yo gonna do some karate moves on me?" He put up his arms in a mocking stance. "Come on, Papa is gonna teach you a lesson you ain't never gonna forget."

I looked around the empty streets. Where the hell were bystanders or cops when you needed them? For crying out loud, that was the whole point of living in one of the most densely populated places in the world.

I stood firm, the tip of my umbrella on the ground like a cane. "You're going to have to come to me."

He laughed and came at me.

I exhaled, then ducked low and launched myself at his torso. I kicked forward between his legs.

He went down.

I pressed the tip of my umbrella against his jugular.

His eyes widened, then rolled in the back of his head, fear, confusion, and angry shame in his face. If he had a gun, I'd be totally screwed.

Time to make sure he wasn't going to come after me. "Stay the fuck away from me." I smacked him across the face with the umbrella and kicked him in the balls for good measure.

He screamed as I stepped around his prone figure and ran for the subway.

————

The Upper West Side was usually bustling at night, but something about the sudden cold and rain kept people from the streets.

I headed toward the block where Hunter's building was located. I had been trying to figure out what I would say to my supposed betrothed, what I could offer him in negotiations. If what he'd said was true, that he too had grown up here on Earth, there was no reason to think he wasn't railing against his potential loss of freedom.

Though not natives, dragons were some of the most magically powerful beings on Earth. It was rumored they could make portals to other dimensions and teleport at will—two abilities long lost to the shen. In addition, they had brought technology far more advanced than anything that had existed on Earth.

So, it made no sense someone that magically powerful would agree to be betrothed to me, a shen with no magic of her own.

Unless Hunter didn't know.

The lump in my chest hardened.

I wouldn't put it past my grandmother, the old fox. The

agreement had been made when I was still an infant, well before the age of manifestation.

If he knew what I truly was, would he still help me? Did my grandmother expect me to marry him under the false pretense that I had my powers? Wouldn't that have just led to one pissed-off dragon?

The question was moot because I wasn't going to go through with this betrothal. But I still needed Hunter's protection.

What could I offer him that he would want?

Something yanked me backward. I flailed, trying not to fall. I looked up and found the girly-yo guy who had tried to stop me before. I took a step back. There was no way a human could have followed me. He glared at me. There was an almost imperceptible green tinge to him. "I'm not done with you."

He smiled with sharp pointed teeth that hadn't been there before. "We've been searching for you for a long time. The fox is stubborn, but we knew she would bring us to you."

Cold dread coated my skin. He had been human once but was now a flesh puppet controlled and piloted by the Devourer.

The man took another grinning step toward me, likely expecting me to turn and run. I extended my umbrella as I screamed and charged, taking him by surprise. He held his arms up, protecting his face from the coming blow.

I ducked and hit him in the legs.

His knees buckled, and he crashed to the cement.

"Hey," I heard him yelling. "The black bitch stole my wallet!"

Blood pounded in my head as I scanned the streets, dreading the sound of sirens or the appearance of a trigger-happy cop. I ran. I ran with everything I had, years and years of track and training all for the inevitable day I'd have to use it.

I sprinted across six lanes of traffic, ignoring the shrieks of the horns. I looked back to see the man stuck on the other side. I was on Hunter's block. I just had to get to his building. Dragons always had some sort of invisible protections on their domains, which would extend to the land it was built on. All I had to do was cross the threshold.

I ran, this time not looking back, dashing as hard as I could, the contents of my backpack bouncing as I shoved my way into the double doors of the gilded foyer.

Classical music played, intermingling with the gentle trickling of a fountain and a doorman who didn't even look up from his phone. From the tinny sound of laser swords and dramatic music, he was in the middle of watching a movie.

I sought to catch my breath, leaning against the wall, until the doorman finally deigned to speak to me. "You got a package?" he asked, still not looking at me.

"What?" I remembered the backpack I wore and realized he must have thought I was a messenger. "No, I'm here to see Hunter."

The doorman gave me an irritated glance, pausing his movie mid-explosion. "Just a second."

It seemed like an eternity passed while the doorman called. I kept my gaze on the glass doors, waiting for the man to show up.

"It doesn't seem like he's in." He went back to his smartphone's screen, and immediately, I heard pew-pew laser guns.

The words punched me in the stomach. I didn't realize how much I had been relying on Hunter to be there, until he wasn't. "Do you know what time he'll be back?"

The doorman shrugged. "Could be today, could be tomorrow."

Fuck. "Do you have his number?"

He sighed, pausing the movie again. "Leave a message." He set a pen and a pad of paper on the counter in front of me and resumed the movie.

I picked up the pen and froze. What would I say to him?

Hi, I need help, come rescue me.

Fuck no. That wasn't me.

Hunter. When you have time, let's talk. Here's my new number.

I wrote the note, slid the pad back to the doorman, and stopped. I retrieved the pad.

Just in case my phone gets broken again, here's my email.

The doorman put the note on top of his desk. "I'll make sure he gets it."

I looked back at the dark, cold, wet streets, and thought of the man lying in wait.

I turned back to the doorman. "Can you call a cab for me?"

The doorman frowned and was clearly about to throw me out.

"Come on," I said, trying a different tack. "Do you think any cab is going to stop for me if I try to hail them at this time of night?"

His glare didn't change. I didn't blame him; the movie sounded like it was just getting to the good part.

"I'm happy to tell you what happens next. They make it to the planet and realize—"

He picked up the phone. "Okay, already. I'll get you a cab."

5

A cab ride to a twenty-four-hour used car lot in Queens resulted in a functional, if beat up, old Honda that still smelled of onions. After a four-hour, nerve-wracking, barely-deer-avoiding, drive to the forests of upstate New York, I pulled up to gravel driveway. My high beams flashed on the massive stone lions flanking the open driveway. I stopped at the invisible line where my grandmother's land began, rolled down the window, and yelled into the dark.

"Mack and Jack, wake up. It's me."

The eyes of the stone lions flared red in response. They stretched, bowed, and then resumed their position.

With the protections activated, I continued onto the gravel and parked beside the back-porch door of the cabin.

Wooden wind ornaments I'd made at camp when I was twelve chimed, and I opened the door. The scent of night-blooming jasmine hit me. Tears filled my eyes as I flicked on the lights. Vines of Grandma's favorite tropical plant had twined upward and over the trellises. Of all the treasures she had amassed over the centuries—scrolls, jewelry, silks—the cutting from the plant had been one of the few things she'd rescued while fleeing the place of my birth. The childhood scent of my summers enveloped me, that of oranges mingled with jasmine.

Immediately inside the cabin, a rose floral couch was paired with a faded blue oriental rug. On a scratched-up coffee table, a laminated crayon-drawing-turned-placemat I'd made in second grade sat next to a faded copy of a Nancy Drew novel.

I dropped my bag by the door and exhaled.

Finally. Safety.

I headed over to the carved rosewood side table, where a bowl of oranges in blue-and-white china sat, flanked by two incense burners filled with ash. Above the table, a scroll of a painted tree reached to the top of the thirty-foot ceiling, with the names of my ancestors scrawled upon it.

But at the very bottom of the scroll, at my eye-level, were the names of the parents I had never known.

I reached into the drawer for matches and lit the incense in greeting and memory and then watched the slender white smoke threads spiral upward.

"Hi, Mom. Hi, Dad."

Incense was only lit for the dead. I did not light one for Grandma. She was still alive somewhere.

She had to be.

The brown plaid couch creaked as I sank into it. I glanced at my phone for the thousandth time. The bars of service kept moving between one and none. I'd forgotten how terrible cell service was up here. With every ping alert on my phone, I kept hoping it was Hunter, but it never was: bill reminders, payment notifications, restaurant recommendations; all I kept getting was stupid stuff that didn't matter. And it wasn't like the cabin had Wi-Fi; Grandma had been planning to add it this summer.

I grabbed a pillow and wrapped my arms around it.

I was not going to cry.

But even as I vowed not to, I could feel tears streaming down my cheeks.

It was all my fault.

And the Devourer was still out there.

My stomach churned with a bone-chilling cold.

Grandma was one of the greatest of our kind. She had outlasted dynasties and outlived all her children and grandchildren, except me. And now she, like my parents, was going to die because of me.

I picked up the laminated drawing. We were making cupcakes together. In the sky, my parents stood on a cloud, smiling.

I placed the drawing face-down on the table. I was ashamed to look at it. Ashamed to face my grandmother. Ashamed to be what I was.

Grandma wouldn't have run. She wouldn't be looking for some random guy to save her. No, she would have laughed, waved her hands, and turned him into a frog or something.

I stared at a knot in the wooden floor, the one that looked like an ugly dog, and willed myself not to cry. This cabin was probably the last refuge of my grandmother's power. Grandma's magic wasn't just limited to what she could do physically but included the self-sustaining magical algorithms she could build into ordinary objects. It was a rare ability, even among shen. Like a house with electricity, I could turn on and off light switches but wiring the house? Generating the power? That was beyond me.

This house could be all I had left of her.

I took a shaky breath. I wasn't leaving this place. Ever since I had been young, she had drilled into me what I was to do in the event something happened to her: come to this cabin and wait.

"Wait for assistance," Grandma had always said.

But then a thought struck me—who was I waiting for help

from? Somehow, she had left that part out. And why had I never thought to ask?

When my magic didn't manifest, more than a few shen who were left shunned us, afraid they might "catch" my disability. Not all of them but enough to hurt.

I wanted to scream. Grandma and her always so-secret plans. I cursed my selfishness, thinking of the message I had left for Hunter. I couldn't drag him into this. I couldn't let another person die protecting me.

I stood up and moved around the room, holding up the phone like a talisman hoping to get just a few more bars. Still nothing.

I sank back into the couch.

I hated this, hated the fact I was just waiting for someone to fucking come and save me.

I walked back to the bowl of oranges and picked one up. A gasp slipped from my lips. Green mold covered the underside.

My grandmother's magic kept the jasmine blooming and the oranges fresh. She wouldn't have let the oranges mold, not unless...

I'd begun to lower the orange back into the bowl when a knock at the door made me jump. I dropped the orange on the lip of the bowl, and in my efforts to catch it, I knocked over the entire vessel. Pieces of delicate porcelain shattered as oranges, all partially furred with green mold, rolled across the floor.

Alarm thudded through my veins. There should be no way anyone reached the door without tripping a ward alarm.

But the wards had remained silent.

I grabbed my umbrella from the stand and asked, "Hello?"

The knocking stopped.

I swallowed, went to the door, turned on the porch light, and looked out the peephole.

No one was there.

"Mack, Jack," I called, my voice shakier than I expected. "Anything out there?"

The distinct sound of heavy thumps came from the back of the house.

I ran to the back door, pulled back the curtains, and turned on the backyard lights, even as terror of what I would find flooded my veins.

Nothing. There was *nothing*.

"Mack? Jack?"

No response.

I called their names again.

Something exploded toward the front of the house. I ran back to the door, glanced through the peephole again, and saw the glowing, crumbled remains of the two stone lions.

I tightened my grip on the umbrella, hot tears streaming down my cheeks. Mack and Jack weren't even alive, just magically programmed constructs. But I had known them all my life, had decorated them with plastic leis and cheap Mardi Gras necklaces when I was six.

I should have felt sorrow. Fear would have been a more rational emotion.

But my family was gone; my grandmother was gone; all because of me, and all I had left of them was this place and my anger.

More thumps banged in the back.

I made sure the front door was locked, went to the rear of the cabin, and turned on the back porch lights, half expecting to see nothing.

At the boundaries of the wards, a crowd of shrouded semi-human figures with glowing eyes, stared back at me.

I closed the curtains and turned my back, bracing myself against the wall, angling my shaking umbrella across my body.

Well, those things were almost certainly not the help I was looking for.

Wait, why was my umbrella shaking? I looked at my hands and realized it wasn't my umbrella. It was my hand, trembling.

My heart was pounding preternaturally fast. Grandma's wards would hold against whatever those things were. They had to hold until help arrived.

Across the room, the incense curled around my father's name. Stormmaker. Lightning had obeyed him, and the thunderclap he'd made with his wings had shattered buildings.

He would never have cowered like this. Nor would my mother or my grandmother.

I dove for the trunk that served as a coffee table, unlocked it, and flung open the lid to find a gray vest and gray gloves inside. I put those on, along with steel-like metal vambraces. There were black shin guards, and I tugged those onto my legs.

At the bottom of the trunk lay a sheathed sword with its pommel partially melted, but the blade was still functional.

It had been my father's. I could use it to bargain with Hunter.

I picked up the umbrella and headed for the back door. Slowly, I walked toward the back, and smelled something... burning. It smelled awful, industrial and chemical.

The shadow things were testing the wards, burning themselves out against the invisible barrier with tiny little sparks.

The wards were too spread out. To intensify their strength against these things, I had to shrink them back.

Which would bring those things even closer.

I swallowed, putting my hand on the cabin walls. "Move back."

Grandma's magical programming was way better than some of the smart-houses being built, allowing even someone like non-magical me to manipulate her wards. The barrier shrank, but as it did, the walls strengthened. Now the shadows huddled closer, having taken a more solid human form but with bald skulls and glowing eyes. I didn't know exactly what they were, but I didn't need to: the wards were built with the Devourer's magic in mind.

Something huge landed in the darkness beyond the shadows.

The shadows turned, swarming into the darkness.

Fire erupted, blindingly bright.

I shut my eyes, willing my vision to return.

A massive, five-toed black reptilian claw emerged from the darkness, followed by a large, smoking snout and bright golden eyes. The black dragon stepped fully into the light. He was as big as a bus, his tail twitching. He watched the cabin with a golden gaze.

Was this the help that was supposed to come?

Was it Hunter?

I unlocked and opened the door. Smoke and bits of swirling ash filled the air.

I took a step out of the cabin. Steam hissed from the dragon's scales as rain began to fall.

It really was a dragon.

My family was made up of fantastical creatures of human mythology. Mermaids, firebirds, unicorns, I had met, and if I had been whole, I would have been just like one of them.

And yet, seeing a dragon, for the first time, was another experience altogether.

The dragon blurred, scales sliding and reforming.

They weren't of this world; they weren't like us shen.

Hunter stood there in human form.

Surrounded by darkness, the mortal, affable façade of the man I had joked about Hoboken with seemed to have vanished. His dark hair was slickening from the rain. His shoulders, his arms, his torso body was so cut, so chiseled, he was basically the manifestation of masculine perfection. Steam hissed when it hit his flesh as it had the dragon's scales, surrounding him. Some drops slid down his very naked body, and I told myself I was keeping my eyes on his face to be appropriate, but the truth was, I was captured by that golden gaze. His look was so intense, there had to be magic behind it.

But dragons didn't do that kind of mental hypnosis magic, did they? As a shen, I should be immune to such tricks, but then again, I was no proper functioning shen.

I swallowed, my mouth as dry as my hair was wet.

I knew what I looked like to him with my mismatched armor and umbrella—like a drowned rodent.

"You're not easy to find," he said.

"How did you do it?"

"Magic," he replied with a straight face.

I gave him a look of disbelief.

The corners of his mouth turned up, and it was like the sun had come out. "You expect me to say something else?"

Something huge and four-footed leapt from the shadows, launching itself at Hunter's back.

"Watch out," I screamed, even as I knew it was too late.

6

I HAD NEVER SEEN A DRAGON FIGHT.

He moved with the quickness of a shen, turning and punching the beast in the side of its head to bring it down. It was no natural thing of this world, with a flat, round rubbery face and rows and rows of serrated teeth. Its tiny eyes and scaled tail brought to mind a strange cross between a shark, wolf, and a lizard.

The thing scrambled to get to its feet, but Hunter had put his foot on its side, holding it in place. He brought another fist down on the thing's neck. The crack resounded through the yard.

The air filled with unearthly squeals.

Two more shark-wolves dashed from the darkness. He picked up the corpse of the thing on the ground. It burst into flames as he swung it. One of the shark-wolves dodged, but he hit another, and it ignited.

I couldn't stand by and let him do this on his own. No one else should die for someone as useless as me. I ran to the edge of the barrier. "Hey! I'm over here!"

Three shark-wolves ran for me.

Hunter yelled, but more leapt toward him and blocked his path to me.

The three shark-wolves snapped and crashed into my grandmother's invisible barrier.

"Hold," I said.

The wards solidified, suspending the shark-wolves in midair. They struggled and hung there, snapping with massive rows of teeth. Tentacles tipped with tiny mouths extended from the shark-wolves' throats, like eyeless glistening eels.

I took Grandma's umbrella and mentally focused on the switch she had made for me. It shimmered into a black sword. I swung it and cut through them in an instant.

Task accomplished, the sword reformed itself into an umbrella.

I glanced back at Hunter. There were shark-wolf bodies strewn around his feet. He stepped over them and came to the barrier, stopping in front of me.

"Come in," I said. The barrier shimmered an opening, and Hunter stepped inside. He was wet, naked, and splattered with shark-wolf gore, yet an irrational heat surged forth at his nearness. I closed the barrier behind him.

Behind us, I heard squeals. I turned to see shark-wolf bodies being seized and dragged away by others of their brethren.

"I didn't mean for you to come." Heat radiated from him like fire turned flesh. He hadn't been that hot before. But then again, there was no need for him to keep anymore dragon secrets from me.

Except his heat made me all too aware of exactly where he was.

"Well, I'm here," he said, as the door clicked shut behind him.

My face flushed warm. I was alone in Grandma's cabin with him, the man who was my betrothed, who I'd almost slept with.

Who was also walking quite naked.

The odd stench of bitterness and oil hit me.

Naked and covered in shark-wolf guts, I reminded myself.

I carefully kept my back to him. "You probably want to rinse off. There's a shower here," I said, heading for a small hallway.

"I'd appreciate that," he replied, his voice close behind me.

I opened the linen closet, trying my best to ignore his proximity. "You don't need to stay. Everyone who has ever tried to protect me has been taken by the Devourer. My parents. And now, my grandmother." I finally found what I was looking for, and I grabbed the towel from the shelf and closed the door a little too loudly. "There's no need for you to add yourself to the list. And I have other backup help coming."

I turned and nearly walked right into him. He grabbed my wrists to keep me from falling, the heat of his hand sending a warm shiver through my skin. "I *am* the backup help. The agreement is still unbroken. You are still my betrothed."

Oh. Hunter *was* the help I was supposed to be waiting for.

He had his hand on the doorknob to the bathroom. Had this hallway always been so small? I shook my head. "You don't need to play the valiant hero card with me."

"I'm trying to help you."

I handed him the rolled-up towel and started to walk away. "Take a shower, I'll make you some tea, then we'll talk."

A strange thought occurred to me. "Hunter," I said, turning around and looking him in the face for the first time since he'd entered Grandma's cabin.

His steady gaze was almost too much for me to take. "Yes, Sophie?"

I couldn't deny there was something between us. But even I knew there were things he wasn't telling me. "How did you know my grandmother was taken?"

His lips turned up in a tight smile. "That release of power? I think every living dragon and shen on the Eastern Seaboard was aware when she was taken," he said, before opening the door to the bathroom.

I headed toward the kitchen, clenching my fists.

Every living shen had been aware except for me. And no one would contact me or help me because they took it as fact that magic-less me would be the next victim of the Devourer.

I let the water run for a few minutes before filling the electric kettle and switching it on. I wondered what kind of tea he would like. Something bold and spicy, I guessed. I picked a chai, and the scent of cloves and cinnamon filled the space. I focused on the act of setting up the teapot with the strainer, pouring the hot water, and setting out the cups on the tray. The simple actions reminded me of her, and even now, it was as if I could hear her beside me saying something like, *It is never not time for tea.*

I splayed my hands on the speckled laminate countertop, imagining I could feel her magic embedded in the surface, as I knew it was.

As always, I felt nothing.

Hunter came into the kitchen, the pink towel with a smiling cartoon cat in a pink dress with a bow on one ear wrapped around his waist. His hair was wet, and his skin was still damp. I had been trying to make him less fucking sexy, but seeing him with that towel emphasizing that V, that torso, I knew I'd never look at Nihao Cat in the same way again.

"Nihao Cat?" he asked with a raised eyebrow.

"What? It's not manly enough for you? I'll make sure I have something black with skulls next time."

"Next time." From his tone, I wasn't sure if he was agreeing or speculating.

I poured some tea into a cup and pushed it toward him. "There's milk and sugar on the tray."

"I'll have it black, thank you."

Of course, he would. He leaned against the wall, in the Nihao Cat towel, his folded arms emphasizing his definitely-not-ordinary biceps, the teacup almost laughably miniscule in his hands. "You know you can't stay here."

I walked past him toward the couch, where I sat and opened the trunk. "This is my grandmother's place. I'm safer here than anywhere else."

"And when the monster finally kills her, her protections will not just be weakened but vanish, leaving you vulnerable."

Tears sprang to my eyes. He thought Grandma was still alive.

I swallowed hard. Of course, she was. She had to be.

Hunter must have seen the raw emotion in my face; he poked at something in the air. There was a brief shimmer of magic. "This wouldn't be here if she wasn't."

Grandma had made sure that help would come for me.

But what about her? Who was going to help her?

I picked the umbrella up off the floor, and, for a moment, felt the weight of the vambraces on my forearms. I had on more enchanted objects than a book of fairy tales. But then, I thought of the rows and rows of yellow teeth. That wasn't even the monster itself but the minions that belonged to it.

I put the umbrella back on the ground. I had no power to rescue her, no power to help anyone.

I finally admitted to myself what I had hoped would happen. I thought it would be other Shen coming to my aide in reconciliation. I clenched my fists. I should have known. Shen protect only themselves. To them, I was no true shen.

And now I had Hunter, my betrothed dragon, come to save me against helpless odds.

The thought of Hunter being consumed by the Devourer seized something in my chest.

"This place is all I have left of her. I'm staying here."

Hunter set the teacup down and strode over to me. "I

assumed, as the daughter of Yifan and the Maker of Storms, this is something you wouldn't let go."

I clenched my fists. "If there was something I could do about it, I would."

He sat down next to me, the couch creaking under his weight.

"You thought I was playing shen games, but I don't play those. Unlike my grandmother, I don't have the capacity to deal with the consequences if I lose."

Hunter frowned.

"I am my mother and father's daughter, and I am shen." I took a deep breath. "But I have no ability to use the power of my heritage."

This was the sort of thing shen would keep under wraps in making a bargain if they could; Grandma apparently hadn't disclosed my non-magical status when she'd arranged my betrothal, after all. Giving him, a dragon, this information without expectation of an exchange was reckless, I knew, but I was tired of secrets.

I said, looking at him, "I am shen, but I wield as much magic as a human."

He looked back with an evaluative gaze.

"An average human," I said, remembering my witchy roommate Chloe.

"The potential is in her blood," he said, repeating my grandmother's words to me. His eyes narrowed. "You commanded your grandmother's wards. You used a magical sword to slay the Devourer's minions. You're wearing what I'm assuming is magical armor. And yet, you claim you cannot use magic."

"I can drive a car too, but that doesn't mean I know how it works or how to build one."

He shook his head.

I looked him in the eye. "I'm not trying to dissuade you or lie to you—"

He reached for my wrist. Heat emanated from his hand, enveloping my arm in flame. I yanked my arm back, but I was no match for his strength.

Instead of burning my flesh, the fire was hot yet oddly pleasant.

An internal warmth began to kindle within me, responding to his flame. "What are you doing?" I asked, my voice oddly breathy.

Fire danced up my arm. It felt like Hunter was caressing my skin, even as my sleeve remained unburned. His eyes were dark, his full lips slightly parted. "Give me your other hand."

That strange feeling within me was warming and responding. I would be foolish not to be wary.

I stopped fighting. But I didn't extend my hand.

"Please," he said, his voice softer. "I promise I won't hurt you. I won't do anything without your consent."

"*Dragons rarely asked for things*," Grandma had once said. And when they did, it was important to listen. Because it meant that you had something they wanted. And dragons almost always got what they wanted. That was where one had to be wary.

And right now, if he and I were fully human, there would be no doubt in my mind as to what he wanted.

But he was not human, and it would be a mistake for me to think of him that way.

I slowly raised my hand and placed it in his. His fingers closed around mine, and the flames shot up my other arm, completing the connection. I gasped as I fully comprehended for the first time what being a dragon meant.

Power.

7

I JUMPED UP AND BACKED AWAY FROM HIM. EVEN SO, THE INTENSITY of his magic was beyond anything I had ever even imagined. It curled around me, calling to the tiny flame within me. My knees started to feel weak, and Hunter stood and caught me in his strong arms before pulling me back down to the couch. His fire burned around us, hot and protective.

I kept babbling, kept talking because I didn't know what else to do. "Yes, it's in my blood because I am still shen. But just because you have eyes doesn't mean you can see. It's like that. I can't use the magic." I stopped and realized something totally inane, but I seized on it because I didn't want to face the magnitude of what I had just admitted to him. "Wait, you're on fire, but the couch isn't"

There was glint of humor in his eyes. "It doesn't burn because I don't want it to." His big hands closed around mine. "There *is* magic in you," said Hunter. "And it will fulfill the bargain that was made, regardless of whether or not you know how to access your power."

His words reminded me of what he really wanted. Not me.

My magic. I said with as much resolution as I could, "I am not marrying you, Hunter."

His fingers tightened around mine. "Not even if it meant defeating the monster and rescuing your grandmother? I can sense your magic. It's locked behind a barrier. I can break it."

I knew what he was getting at. "I'm not letting you seal me to you."

He looked at me. "What do you know about the sealing process?"

I pulled away from him and rose from the couch. "It's a magical bond that allows for control over a person being sealed. I don't care what your intentions are, I'm not going to be anyone's minion or magical sex puppet."

He stopped, leaning back on the couch, the corners of his lips turned upward. "Minion? Magical sex puppet? Really? What kind of stories have you shen been telling about us? Do you think we are so like the Devourer?" He shook his head. "Sealing does create a bond between two people. And yes, there are times in which there is one partner more fully in control than the other. But it is, as humans say, a two-way street. And it doesn't have to be permanent."

I stopped and sat down in the chair opposite him. This was a much better place, away from him, away from his touch. I closed my eyes and pinched the bridge of my nose. Grandma said she'd sent failed champions against the Devourer, hoping that "it wouldn't come to this," a marriage with a dragon. As a child, how many times had I heard the story of her flight with me, her certainty that she and I were going to die, and the desperate call for help, answered by the most unlikely of allies?

Why had I never even asked her what the bargain was that she had struck with the dragons in exchange for helping us to get to America?

Stupid, stupid, stupid me.

I should have known better.

I opened my eyes., Hunter was leaning back on the couch, arms open, regarding me thoughtfully. Shen and dragon had been at odds since their arrival on Earth. In some respects, shen knew as much about dragons as humans knew of the true nature of shen.

Including the exact nature of what a dragon seal was.

I took a deep breath. "You can't expect me to agree to anything without telling me more about what sealing is."

His smile didn't miss a beat. "I would be able to access your magic and you, mine."

I scrubbed a hand over my face as I stood up and began to pace. Maybe this was her way of trying to give me a chance to be more shen than I was—giving me a chance to access magic in a different form.

"But now that you have been truthful with me, I will be truthful with you, as well. I want you to seal yourself to me because I need your power to destroy the Devourer."

"My 'power?'" I let out a harsh laugh. "There are so many things wrong with your assumptions." I faced him. "First of all, you know your own history, right? The Devourer destroyed your world, your civilization, your armies. How are you going to kill this thing when it turned dragons into refugees?"

There was a grimness and carefully caged fury in his expression that reminded me of a predator, furious at his prey's escape. "The Devourer here on Earth is incomplete. It's only a piece of what it was, and it's been weakened in coming here, cut off from its masters in a place, in a time, it doesn't belong. Earth is our home now. It's my home, and I intend to rid my territory of the threat it poses before it's able to contact the rest of itself."

There. There was that famous territorial dragon instinct.

Wait a minute. Incomplete? The rest of itself? "Are you saying there's more than one Devourer?"

He blinked. "Yes and no. It makes copies of itself and alters its copies for specific purposes. It's possible to kill pieces of the Devourer. We've been doing just that for the last few years."

The words he spoke implied something I'd never believed could be true. "Wait. Are you saying you've gone up against the Devourer and won?"

"Pieces of it. Small pieces."

So, it was possible. I quashed that moment of brightness. "I don't understand why you think you need me."

"Because we are about to go up against the Mother of Teeth, the largest and oldest portion of the Devourer, the one that followed my people through the gates so many years ago."

The same piece that had followed the dragons and killed my parents and countless other shen.

"You're still not answering my question," I said, snatching an orange quilted throw pillow from the couch and squeezing it.

"Because the Devourer learns from its past battles and opponents. But in all this time, the Devourer has never faced dragon and Shen magic working together in a common cause to defeat it. Only separately."

I shook my head. "It's still a suicide mission."

"Perhaps," he admitted, looking away.

He had always known it, I realized. He had already long committed himself to this course of action, well before I had ever crossed paths with him.

When I was young, I'd met a distant aunt who had once been famous for stealing young, handsome warriors and keeping them under her spell until all they'd known turned to dust. When I'd asked her why she'd done such things, she had said, "To prevent them from throwing their lives away in meaningless deaths."

In that moment, I understood Great Aunt Titania.

Springs squeaked as Hunter got off the couch. His hand

closed on mine once more with searing heat. I opened my eyes with a gasp.

Magical flames surrounded us. There was an odd warmth within me, one mingled with desire. No, not wholly desire but something else. Something that had been missing within me my entire life.

His fingers tightened. "You are magic, and even if you don't know how to use it, I do."

I blinked.

"Help me. I would protect you. I would treat you as an equal partner."

The potential is in your blood.

I broke free. The flames around us died and dwindled to nothing. The fire, the heat within me that I had felt while connected to him, was replaced by an all too familiar feeling of anger and self-loathing.

"You say sealing is not slavery. Then, tell me what it is. And why I should believe you."

I saw my laminated childhood drawing.

"It's a bond of magical access." I heard his voice, so close behind me. He said nothing else.

I was giving him too much ground. I turned, planted myself to the floor, and found him absurdly close, so close I could smell the lingering scent of soap on his skin. I was, at once, at war with myself wanting to get close and yet wanting to back away at the same time. "That's all. Isn't there more to it than that?"

He assessed me calmly, the dragon in his eyes watching me. "It's always different, depending on who is involved. No two seals are ever alike, just as no two people are ever alike. Help me, and we may have a chance to help your grandmother."

How selfish was I? What kind of shen was I? He was offering a chance to defeat the monster that had killed my family.

He was still too close, kiss-close. I covered my mouth, then uncovered it, hoping he wouldn't notice. "Do you really think my grandmother is alive?"

He missed nothing, especially how stupidly nervous I was. "If her protections are still here, then yes."

"She designed this place to withstand magical attacks, even after her death."

He looked me up and down, then slowly, deliberately backed away and relaxed back down on to the couch. Still, the dragon was in his eyes, watching me like he expected me to bolt. "The Devourer has spent years building creatures designed to break this place. Even now, it waits and watches."

This was how the Devourer always got what it wanted. Denied its goal, it would plan and bide its time, studying, designing, and building constructs designed to overcome what had stopped it.

I had to stop running. "Do you truly think you can kill the Devourer?"

He leaned back on the couch, sprawling. I'd never thought of the couch as being small, but he definitely made it seem so. "I have before. But not against a piece so centralized. The Devourer has never faced an alliance of dragon and shen magic. With your help, we have a chance."

Here was a man, a dragon, who had accomplished what I thought was impossible.

There was only one thing I could say. But before I agreed to anything, I had to negotiate.

"What about being married to you allows you to tap my magic? Could you do it with just sex, without marriage?" Even as I said it, I could feel my face grow warm.

Hunter's expression was oddly evaluative and otherwise unreadable. "Are you offering yourself to me? Outside of the bonds of marriage?"

"Bonds of marriage," I repeated with a forced levity. "What

century are you from? Didn't we just almost have sex like... yesterday?" It seemed like a lifetime ago.

He narrowed his eyes. "That was different, and you know it. What you're offering is something else."

I folded my arms. "I value my freedom."

He stood up and crossed the room, putting himself in my personal space. "Marriage is not slavery, just as sealing is not slavery."

He was too close, smelled too good. I backed away from him, keeping my arms crossed. "Anything you're forced into without free consent is slavery. Don't you want more from a marriage than just power-sex? Don't you want companionship? Don't you want to get to know the other person? Don't you want to have a choice?"

There was that blank, emotionless face of his, the sort I might expect if he were facing some terrible monster. "What if you had the choice now, Sophie?"

To make a lie believable, you have to lean into it. You have to make yourself believe it, and above all, with men, you have to physically distract them, or at least, that's what Grandma always said. I unfolded my arms, reached out to him, and began lightly tracing a vein up his forearm, around the curve of a thick bicep. "I want to save my grandmother. But I don't want to marry you, Hunter. If sex is what you need, well, that, I can offer."

His hand was on the small of my back. He pulled me to him, and I could feel him hard against my belly.

"I accept." His mouth crushed mine.

Fire roared up within me to meet him, wanting him, needing him to touch me. Desire blazed, but there was more to it than mere lust; something was waking what had slumbered inside me for my entire life. I clung to him and his strong arms, trying not to drown, trying to keep my head in the inferno of sensations that buzzed around me.

Hunter's voice was low and thick against my neck. "I keep my promises, Sophie. I was very clear about my intentions toward you."

A memory of him vowing to taste everything flashed. Hunter chuckled at the goosebumps that covered my skin. His hand slid up my shirt. My voice trembled as I asked, "This sealing isn't going to be permanent, right?"

"Not if you don't want it to be," he replied, undoing my bra. I wanted to purr at his touch and the sound of his voice. Did all dragons have such a voice of promise and seduction or was it just him? He kissed me, and I melted into him as if I'd known him longer than today. Or was it yesterday? The only thing I was sure of was how much I wanted him. "But it will require repetition."

Primal desire for him intoxicated me. One hand slid to my front, cupping my breast, his thumb on my nipple. A spark pinged downward to my core, desire slickening me.

I broke free of his kiss. My fingers climbed the outrageously muscular landscape of his torso. "You don't need to enchant me to get me to have sex with you." My voice was breathy and unrecognizable.

"I don't use magic to coax consent." His fingers tilted my chin upward. The fire was in his eyes, honest and primal. "Never."

I looked away, unable to bear the weight of his gaze.

I fingered the pink towel around his waist. His hand closed around my wrist, holding my palm against him. "Wait," he said. "Not yet."

I had to take advantage of this momentary lull before I truly lost my senses. I attempted to tease him, to regain some measure of control. "Oh, right," I said, hanging a smile on my face. "I haven't asked you for your consent."

He removed the towel and dropped it to the floor, revealing

his very large and obvious consent. Involuntarily, I clenched at the thought of that, of him, inside me.

"Oh," I said.

In the space of a breath, he yanked me to him, crushing me against his chest hard. I opened to him, and his mouth was on mine, his hands peeling off my yoga pants. He splayed his hand on my mound, sliding a thick finger along the cleft. I shuddered at the slide that barely grazed my clit and fought the urge to grind myself against his palm. "You're not going anywhere this time," he rumbled. "Not when you're so wet. Ahh, Sophie, I'm so hard and you're so ready, I could fuck you right now."

His words brought on a surge of needful desire. "Then do it," I said. "Fuck me now, Hunter."

His fingers teased my clit, and I could hear the smile in his voice when he said, "No."

I reached for his cock and wrapped both hands around him. Every one of Hunter's muscles tightened. I had the sense that he was holding himself back with tremendous effort. "What?"

His fingers toyed with the crotch of my panties. "Oh, I have every intention of sheathing my cock in you." He shoved two fingers inside me. "Just not yet."

I gasped at the intimate invasion. His thumb hard against my clit.

And like that, with one hand inside me, he lifted me off my feet in a display of inhuman strength. I tried to steady myself with my arms around his neck, but every movement only drove sparks of hot pleasure through my system until my body convulsed.

Oh, my gods, had I just orgasmed from a few touches of his fingers? Which were actually still inside me...and I was still clenching against him in little aftershocks.

"Stop using your magic," I gasped. "It's not fair."

"I'm not using magic," he said with a satisfyingly smug voice, grabbing my breast with his free hand. He pinched my nipple hard. "You're just fucking hot for me."

Pleasure ricocheted from my breast to my core, and I let out an animalistic moan. His fingers flexed, his thumb rubbed, and I fucking came again.

"You just going to stand there and finger fuck me all night? Does this get you off?"

"Feeling you orgasm on me?" A happy male smile spread across his face. The look in his eyes was toe-curling. "Yeah, actually it does."

His hand was on his cock. I reached down to touch him, but he merely shifted me upward. "No, Sophie, not yet."

"Is the big bad dragon so afraid of a little hand job?"

"Taunt me. Tease me. But you're not denying me this."

With his hand still inside me, he lifted me and set me on his mouth. The unexpected display of his strength, mixed with the insane feeling of his impossibly long tongue flickering against my clit and the shadow of his beard rough against my inner thighs, turned my limbs to jelly. "Hunter!" My voice came out in a breathy plea.

He kept going, his fingers gripping my ass tight, holding me immobile against his mouth. I pulled at his thick, dark hair, and he only laughed and kept going, pressing me harder against his mouth.

I said his name again, and again, moaning it out as his hot mouth melted all my common sense.

Only after I'd come again did Hunter relent but only to a degree. He lowered me to his lap.

I straddled his big body, his cock sliding against my nether lips, grazing my clit.

To say he was thick would have been an understatement.

I savored his naked cock pressed against my most intimate place, a sensation I had never felt before. With my human partners, I always had to do the safe-sex thing with condoms—to avoid questions more than anything else. But shen didn't get human STDS, nor could we pass them on. And pregnancy only came if a shen wished it to be.

The feel of him bare to me was one of the hottest things I had ever experienced.

And by the look in his eyes, Hunter fucking knew it.

"You've only ever been with humans, haven't you?"

"It was always safer that way."

"Safer, yes. Humans have their charms. But you are shen. And I am dragon."

A fluttery panic set within me. Something desperate clawed inside me. He was going to be disappointed—better do it now. "I don't know what you expect. Remember, Hunter, for all intents and purposes, I have as much magic as an average human."

"So you said. Those exact words, actually. We shall see."

"You're going to be frustrated—" I gasped at the sudden sensation of heat caressing my skin with a fervency that mirrored the renewed desire within me.

"I don't use magic to coax consent," he said. "I use it in the way it was meant to be used."

Sparks flew and skittered around my skin. His magic teased me, touching a place within me I hadn't even known was there. I squirmed against him, and the impossible pressure built.

"Please, Hunter," I cried, wanting something I hadn't even known was possible.

He slid a hand underneath my ass, keeping my entrance on the blunt head of his cock as he stood. I tried to take in more of him, but he only held me still, effortlessly overpowering me, and smiled.

"What are you doing?"

"Making sure I don't burn down your cabin."

He carried me to the hallway, where he kicked open the bathroom door.

Then he turned and set me down in the shower and cranked it on.

I screeched in fury as cold water hit my skin.

His mouth was on mine, his body on mine, his fire on mine, the contrast of cold and wet stinging my skin, maddening my hunger. I needed him, needed his magic and his cock inside me, more than anything I'd ever needed in my life.

"Sophie." His voice was hard and guttural with an accent of power. "Look at me."

I wrapped my legs around his waist and gazed into his eyes.

With a hard, brutal thrust, Hunter shoved his cock, his heat, his fire inside me.

Power shot from him and hurtled through me, and I was consumed with pleasure. I clung to him as he stretched me wide, driving into me faster and harder than humanly possible.

And I welcomed it.

I convulsed around him again and again. He'd shift, and my core would clench down on him hard, and then, he'd thrust again and start over.

Impaled against the wall, steam hissed around us, and I could feel his power, his magic thrusting within me, embracing me, licking my virgin magic with a thousand flickers of desire.

He was fierce. He was hot, and I was magnificently full. He began to quicken his pace.

Suddenly, a pressure crowded me, surrounding me, tightening in a space that I had been stuck in all my life. All I wanted was to be free. Power invaded me, unstoppable, immense, delicious.

I reveled in his growing frenzy, in his low, rumbling, inhuman groans. My legs were spread wide and wrapped around him, my heels at the small of his back. I rocked against him. "Please, Hunter, please." I forgot all my pride, begging him because if he didn't start moving faster, I knew I'd go up in flames.

His fire spread to encompass my flesh, the hiss of water on fire, the steam surrounding us. He was in me, around me, a part of me physically and magically in a way that no one had ever been.

And to my surprise, it felt shockingly right.

"You are mine," he said, his mouth against my ear.

I recognized the words — sealing words. I didn't know what I was supposed to say, so I tried a line from a dragon tale I once read. "My fire is yours," I said, the words dropping from my mouth with the heavy weight of magic.

He gave a deep, victorious smile. One I knew I would remember for the rest of my life, no matter what came after.

His big body drove me against the wall, his hips holding me in place.

And he fucked me, incredibly, amazingly slowly, withdrawing before driving back into me so hard, fire burning so hot, my clit vibrating from the hammer of his hips against mine.

The fierce burgeoning detonated within me. I screamed as a startled frenziness rushed through me, through him in a magical surge of flame. Our bliss burned—beautiful, unstoppable, and undeniably ours.

We were power. We were fire. We were magic.

And we were one.

8
_____

"Holy gods, Hunter," I said, taking a colorful rainbow towel from him.

"There are no gods," he replied, quoting a famous ancestor of mine, showing off his knowledge of my family. "Just shen." His undisguised dragon gaze told me he wasn't through with me yet.

Something inside me quivered in hot anticipation.

As I wrapped the towel around me, something cracked in the cabin. Maybe I felt it more than heard it, as true magic didn't have a sound.

Grandma's wards flashed visible.

Oh no.

The words dissolved into nothingness.

Suddenly, I heard her voice in my head.

Little fox, I am proud of you.

She was gone.

No. No. No.

My cheeks were wet. I wiped them with the back of my hand, took a deep breath, and realized I was crying.

Why was I crying? I didn't even know for sure if that was really her or just another random echo I was imagining.

Hunter had the strangest look on his face.

"Your magic." He began to laugh, an odd note in his voice. "You're a Justice."

"A what?" I was listening and speaking at the same time, but all I could think about was that Grandma might be gone.

Something else broke, a sound like rock crumbling. I looked around but couldn't see what it was.

"I didn't even know Earth had Justices."

I felt wrung out. I wiped my cheeks again and took a breath. "What the hell is a Justice?" The rumbling continued. Hunter turned, searching for the source of the ominous sound as he spoke. "In the histories of the world from which we came, there are stories of Justices. Always rare, always feared."

Hunter stopped, and my gaze followed his to the north wall of the cabin. Before our eyes, cracks in the white plaster crawled upward toward the ceiling.

"That doesn't answer my question," I said, unable to take my eyes off the wall.

"Where they walk, people will sicken, the milk will spoil, and good works will crumble to dust," he murmured, quoting something I had no knowledge of. "Dragons hunted Justices to extinction a long time ago."

The cracking on the wall stopped. It shouldn't have happened. I scrambled away from him and picked my clothes off the floor. "What are you talking about?"

"Justices erase magic. Originally, they were known as balance-restorers, those who could reset things to a pre-magic state. Restoring Justice, they called it."

I threw on my bra and then put on my T-shirt. "Why did dragons start hunting them?"

"Over time, dragons began to rely on magic more and more,

building everything with it. Cities, spaceships, hospitals. A Justice became a weapon that the dragon kingdoms used mercilessly against each other. The histories say Justices brought an end to the Golden Age. And so, as a result, they were hunted because they were a weapon thought to be too dangerous to exist."

I took a step back, horror sinking cold teeth into my skin.

He realized I was backing away from him. "I didn't hunt them, Sophie. This was all well before my time."

I shook my head. "No. I can't be. I may not be able to use my own magic, but I've been able to use my grandmother's spells and enchanted objects."

"You said yourself you don't need magic to use those."

I looked at my hands. "If I am an eraser of magic, then why aren't you dead?"

He narrowed his eyes. "Dragon fire is not magic in the way that you think it is."

"Wait, aren't you trying to use me as a magic battery?"

"Shen power is different. Sealing converts it into a form I can use."

I didn't have the power he thought he needed.

I was totally useless to him.

I turned away so he couldn't see my face. I rummaged in the bag from my apartment, and found a pair of jeans, perfect for delaying more action in case I let my hormones get the best of me again. I put them on, swallowing the odd bitterness in my mouth. I had to focus on the problem in front of me.

How could my grandmother have missed what I was?

She wouldn't have.

I reached behind my shoulder, to where her sigil was. I couldn't feel that tingle any longer.

"Your grandmother's sigil. It locked in your power and kept it from disrupting her spells."

He picked something off the ground and handed it to me.

I stared at the black umbrella in my hand, and I knew something fundamental had changed.

I tested a thrust forward.

It remained a normal umbrella.

Oh no.

I jumped off the couch and threw open the trunk. The sword was still there.

His voice came from directly behind me. "I didn't know that was still around."

I pointed to the sword. "Pick it up and tell me if you feel any magic in there."

He looked at me as if I had told him to pick up a scorpion. "It's not going to bite you."

"With what I heard, I wouldn't be surprised."

He took the sword from me and studied the hilt for a moment before setting it down. "It feels like an ordinary non-magical sword to me."

My shoulders sank. It wasn't a touch thing; it was something that had happened during sealing. Apparently, I had just erased the power from one of the last great magical weapons of the shen. Wonderful. I picked up the sword, which felt like what it always felt like to me: an ordinary sword.

"I can identify your magic, but I don't know how the magic of Justices work or how shen magic works," he said. "There might still be magic there."

I set down the sword and moved away from him to open another ottoman; Grandma had a particular love for multi-functional storage furniture. I picked up a leather harness with several sheathed knives and put it on over my shirt. "If I'm a 'justice' as you say, then I guess I can't be your magical battery."

I saw the moment he realized what I was trying to say. I spoke faster to get it over with and occupied myself with strapping the leather harness to my chest. "If I can't be your magical battery, there's no need for us to be betrothed. And no need for you to be here."

His hand was warm on my shoulder. "Sophie, you're in danger. I'm not going to leave you to face it alone."

I knew I should move away from him, but I couldn't bring myself to do it. Still, I couldn't let myself look at him and let him see the turmoil I was struggling to hide. I forced condescension into my voice. "Don't be foolish. If you plan to go up against the Devourer, you undoubtedly have magical items at your disposal. You can't risk bringing me along."

The floor buckled and cracked underneath me, and I stumbled. Instantly, Hunter's arms were around me, steadying me, my back against his chest.

A chorus of unearthly wolf-like howls surrounded the house.

"The Devourer's monsters. They're here," Hunter announced.

"They won't breach the wards."

His arms tightened around me. His voice was strangely gentle. "Sophie. You broke your grandmother's wards."

Something crashed through the window.

With shen-like speed, Hunter picked it up and threw it back outside.

Light and fire erupted. The windows exploded.

I threw my hands up to protect myself, but Grandma's internal shields had already activated around us, keeping us safe. I glanced at the ground, and saw shattered pieces of jagged glass reflected multiples of myself. Grandma would have had a fit at the mess.

I hooked my arm around Hunter's. "Can you fix the wards?"

"No. Shen magic is different."

Fuck. For the millionth time in my life, I cursed my lack of magic.

There was another loud cracking sound, and then, something fell.

Hunter yanked me to him as something crashed behind me. I glanced back and the heavy wood ceiling beam sat in the place where I had been standing before.

His arms held me tightly. "We have to get out of here."

"No." I fought to break free, but he wouldn't release me. "Let me go!" Tears filled my eyes. This place was all that remained of Grandma, all that remained of my family. If I left, I would be leaving them, leaving her, behind.

There was a loud thump on the roof.

Hunter threw me to the ground. In a fast blur, he exploded into a massive black dragon and rose above me, spreading his wings, shielding me from the chunks of wood and green fire suddenly raining down. A cold wind sliced between us.

I was staring at open sky.

The roof had been ripped off

A wall of green mage fire roared around us.

The black dragon that was Hunter made a rattling sound, opening massive jaws to reveal teeth longer than my arms. Something mammalian within me froze in fear, utterly convinced I was about to be eaten.

Fire erupted from the dragon's mouth, hitting something in the sky. There was a haunting, resonating howl.

Then, a massive claw wrapped around me, and the dragon sprung skyward.

I let out a scream as he ripped me from the ground. Just as my stomach caught up with me, I found myself falling onto the grassy lawn outside the remains of my grandmother's burning house. Acrid smoke burned my lungs. Tears blurred my vision, but I could still see it: A barbed arrow the size of a rake piercing the membrane of Hunter's wings, pinning them together.

"Hunter!"

Incomprehensible anger and heat rushed through me. Hunter was hurt because of me. My grandmother had been taken and was either dead or dying because of me. My parents had been killed because of me.

All because of me.

It would be better for everyone if I had never existed.

Claws dug into my armor, knocking me over. The massive jaws of a shark-wolf snapped at my face. I screamed and somehow managed to yank out a knife from my harness, forcing my anger, my frustration, and the knife into the side of the shark-wolf's neck.

Dust went into my mouth and nose, choking me. What the—

I heard the whistling approach of multiple shark-wolves and staggered to my feet.

A pack of them watched me with glowing yellow eyes. Behind me, Hunter roared, and I could hear something screaming and flesh tearing. I knew if I turned to look, I would be dead.

I pulled out another knife from the harness. It would be a good death, to die on my grandmother's land.

"Come at me, then!"

The pack of shark-wolves attacked.

But while I was convinced, I was about to die, it seemed that anger and grief had given me the power to live. Never before could I anticipate my attackers' moves so well, even if they weren't human. Never before did every punch, every kick, every slash land precisely where it needed to. My granduncle, the god of kungfu who'd refused to teach me, might have even deigned to give me a nod of approval.

I fought until all that remained around me was a circle of gray ash.

I held myself alert, ready for the next onslaught, searching the darkness.

And I suddenly realized how quiet it was.

"Hunter?" I looked around and spotted him in human form on his knees. I ran to him. "Hunter! Are you okay?"

Hunter's hand was inside a man's chest. As I approached, Hunter's forearm tighten. The man screamed.

My ancestors had been the monsters and gods of ancient humanity. Some of them had killed, sacrificed, and even eaten humans. Something like this shouldn't have bothered me.

But I had spent too long living among humans.

"Hunter!" I yelled, the horror evident in my voice.

He didn't look at me. Instead, the man's chest began to smoke, and the scent of burnt flesh filled the air. Hunter's voice was grim. "We are coming for you, Devourer."

The man's screams turned to laughter, and its voice changed into something gurgling and not of this world. "Come for me, then, dragon. I await you."

The man's entire body went up in flames.

Hunter glanced up at me, fire still flaring in his hand as he burned away the blood. "The Devourer had already taken control."

I closed my eyes. "I know." I had no cause to criticize, for the shen had been manipulating humans for their own gain as long as humans had existed. But the Devourer ate their personalities, enslaving their minds and bodies turning them into meat puppets. "What about your wings?"

"I'm fine," he said with all the brusqueness of a man who didn't want to talk about his pain.

With shen, injuries suffered in one form carried over to other forms. But was it the same with dragons? Even though they, like shen, walked in human form, dragons were quite literally aliens from another world.

There was a crash behind me, and I turned to see a wall of the cabin collapsing, green flames eating away at the timbers even as the walls tried futilely to rebuild. It was a testament to the brilliance of Grandma whose magical algorithms sought to protect themselves even as they were being destroyed. I dropped to my knees, sorrow wrapping itself around my throat.

I couldn't even protect myself or my grandmother's house.

In the trees, a flash of high beams blazed, and I heard a vehicle coming along the dirt road, fast.

Hunter's hand was on my back. "Sophie, our ride is here."

I was frozen, unable to tear my eyes away from the burning green flames engulfing the cabin.

"All I have left of my family is there," I said. "My grandmother's place is gone. My father's sword is gone. My entire childhood —all of it, gone."

A massive black SUV pulled up. The window rolled down. The driver had a lion-like blond mane with shoulders and biceps that bulged almost obscenely from the sleeves of his gray T-shirt. But there was that particular fire in his eyes that said he was no shen. "Hey," the man said to Hunter. "It's a bitch to find this place."

"It's meant to be," he replied. "Sophie, Lucas. Lucas, Sophie. Both of you stay here. I'll be back in a moment."

He headed toward the flames.

Wait, what was he doing? "Hunter!"

He didn't even turn; he just kept going as he called back, "Dragon, remember?"

I stared at the burning building. "It's mage fire!"

Green flames embraced his naked form. "A dragon fears no fire."

Mage fire was said to be another creation of the Devourer's. But as with the shen, sometimes, stories were wrong.

"I thought mage fire was designed to kill dragons," I said to myself.

Lucas, who had gotten out of the SUV, came to stand next to me.

"It is." Luca stared at the angrily burning cabin, the fire alive and roaring, "We have some protection from mage fire, but it generally feels like being eaten alive by a colony of fire ants. Ones that are actually magical and on fire. Whatever he's going in there for must be important."

Yup, Lucas was definitely another dragon.

Time slowed, and it felt like hours passed.

Suddenly, the house shuddered and crumpled into a pile, and flying sparks filled the air.

NO. "Hunter!" I tried to run toward the house but found a large male hand clamped around my wrist. "Let me go!"

"Wait," said Lucas. "Look."

I yanked my wrist away and turned toward the green flames. There was an odd flicker of red flame. The flicker became a figure, a tall, bright figure of red and yellow fire, striding out of the emerald inferno, which snarled around him a dozen green tentacles.

The figure had a bright, gleaming sword in his hand.

Flames licked his splendidly naked human form, outlining his broad shoulders and bulging muscles. His eyes glowed and fire flared from him, a living god of fire.

No, I reminded myself, he was no shen, and I would be a fool to ever forget that.

I wanted to run to him, to hug him, but I was suddenly aware of Hunter's glorious nakedness and Lucas's presence.

He stopped in front of me. "I'd hand you the sword now, but you should wait for it to cool."

I balled my fingers into fists because if I didn't, I'd end up touching him. "Why did you do that? It's nothing but an ordinary sword now."

His gaze was full of meaning. "Just because something doesn't have magic doesn't mean it's not of value."

"Hey," said Lucas, his voice slightly bored. Clearly, he was used to picking up naked and dirty people from in front of a flaming building in the middle of the night on a regular basis. "You both can keep eye-fucking each other in the back seat. Let's get out of here."

Hunter shot him a dirty look. Lucas ignored him, opened the back passenger door, and gestured me in. I slid into wonderfully heated black leather and set the sword on the floor of the car. Lucas closed the door, and Hunter opened the door on the other side.

"There's the duffel with clothes back there."

"Got it," Hunter replied.

I looked out the window towards the burning cabin, as the SUV started. "Are we really going to just leave a magical fire burning in the middle of the woods?"

"Mage fire will die quickly without the presence of dragons," Hunter explained as he unzipped his bag. "Any news?"

Lucas sighed. "When the Devourer took the kitsune, she left a magical trail that was basically a map to the Devourer's base. Daniel confirmed the base."

Grandma. I looked out the window. I couldn't believe I was really leaving the cabin.

"Is she still alive?" I asked.

"Unclear," said Lucas. He paused. "Though before this piece of the Devourer went dormant a decade ago, it liked to keep those it took alive for experiments."

I closed my eyes and swallowed hard. I had forgotten about that. Another one of the many rumors spread by the remaining shen about the Devourer. It had no form, nor was it invisible. It was all-seeing. It could read your mind, predict your actions, experimented on its prisoners, and so on and so forth. The Devourer was the stuff of nightmares but real.

Maybe it would be better if Grandma was gone.

The thought loomed in my mind like a gathering storm. I would cry if I thought anymore about it, and I didn't want to cry in front of them.

So, I changed the subject. "Who is Daniel?"

"Another member of our small group."

"How many of you are there?"

"Four," Hunter said at the same time Lucas said, "Three."

"Lana is not going to be a part of this," Lucas snapped, with ice in his voice. "She's human."

"That doesn't mean she's not important."

There was a low, warning rumble from the front seat. I got the feeling they'd had this discussion before.

Hunter's hand covered mine. "I'm working with friends, and we're going to find the Devourer and end its existence. We'll find a place for you, Justice or not. We'll figure out how to help you."

"I don't understand how you think three dragons can succeed where an army of dragons failed," I said.

"Whoa, whoa, whoa," Lucas interjected. "Did you just call her a Justice?"

"Yes," Hunter.

"A Justice," said Lucas repeated. He was silent for a moment. "Well, that calls for a change of plans. I'll let Daniel know he needs to hide the magical silver."

"Magical silver?" Silver was inherently not magical. Actually, it was the exact opposite and repelled magic.

Like me, I suppose. Apparently, I was the equivalent of shen silver.

Lucas kept talking. "You know how humans have a saying to

hide the silver. We're gonna have to hide the magic weapons so you don't erase them."

Hunter shook his head. "Lucas hasn't spent as much time in human society as I have."

"That was a very nice attempt at humor," I said.

Lucas groaned. "Even I know that's sarcasm. So, I hear you're a practitioner of Krav Maga. Why Krav Maga? Wasn't your granduncle the god of Shaolin Kungfu or something?"

That much was common knowledge among the shen. What wasn't as well-known was exactly what he thought of me. I gave the easy answer, cloaked in enough truth to be believable. "Yes, but he's not the god of subways. The Krav Maga studio was an easier subway trip on the R."

"Has Daniel figured out where the menace is hiding?" asked Hunter as he threw on a shirt.

"An island in the Caribbean. It owns it through an array of shell companies, but Lana was able to track it down. The sat images of the compound are in the tablet back there."

Hunter pulled out the tablet from the pocket behind the front seat and swiped at the screen. He angled it toward me. "Do you want to see where the Devourer is?"

I took the tablet from him. There was a sprawling complex of white rectangles on a small island surrounded by a crystalline blue sea. It was the complete opposite of where I had imagined the Devourer would hide.

I handed the tablet back to Hunter and looked out the window. He wasn't my only option. Though the number of shen relations I knew I could actually rely on were less than the number of people in this vehicle. Finding them would be another journey in itself. In the past, they had always come to Grandma.

Grandma.

I tried to stifle the sudden clench of pain and bitterness in my throat. Hunter and Lucas started talking about their plan of attack, and I knew I should have been paying attention. Maybe it was the aftermath of the magic and exhaustion—maybe it was Lucas's terrible driving—but the weird roiling in my belly made me feel like I was going to throw up. I closed my eyes to concentrate on not embarrassing myself in front of Hunter.

9

White noise surrounded me, yet Hunter's voice seemed to cut through it all. "No, I didn't feel any different."

Another male voice spoke, "Are you sure she's a Justice?"

I blinked and realized I lay horizontal on a couch, with a warm gray blanket over me.

"She blew out the internal wards of the kitsune's den. She literally turned the avatars of the Devourer into dust. When I went back into the cabin, the plants that had not burned were withered and the magics that held the den together literally faded from existence."

I looked around at polished wood, grey leather seating, and the tell-tale row of small porthole windows lining curved walls. An omnipresent hum of white noise filled the background.

I went to a window and saw lights far below us in the dark, clouds hovering by.

The other male spoke again. "That could be useful."

Voices lowered, and there was more discussion that I couldn't hear. I scanned around me. This really was a plane. A private deluxe jet by the looks of it, with the expensive hallmarks of the same interior decorator at Hunter's place.

His voice cut through the white noise again. "Not like this."

I stood up and walked toward the voices, passing a divider. Around a large brown conference table, Hunter and Lucas sat, along with another man with light-brown skin who looked like he should be strutting down catwalks in Milan.

Next to the unknown man was another woman, her skin a lighter shade of brown than mine, her dark hair tied back into a ponytail. She wore a gray Wellesley sweatshirt. In front of each of them was a laptop, a tablet, and a phone. There was a dizzying array of cables, wires, and devices in the middle of the conference table—some technological, some clearly not of this world.

They all looked up at me.

I gaped at Hunter in disbelief. "A private jet? Really? Who are you guys, Batman?"

"Batman is singular, not plural. Also, he works alone, and doesn't fly, and doesn't have superpowers," said Lucas.

"Thank you, Mr. Comic Book Dictionary," Hunter retorted, getting out of his seat.

"Hi," said the girl who waved to me from across the table. "I'm Lana, the human."

"Like Clark Kent's hometown girl crush," added Lucas, suddenly fascinated by the buttons on his wrist.

Lana rolled her eyes at Lucas. "You must be the fairy princess."

I blinked. Fairy, fae, demon, devil: humans had many words for us. As different as we looked, ultimately, we were all shen. And we had no royalty in the way of human rankings. I inhaled deeply, tired of checking off another box for the convenience of human understanding. "Um, sure," I said. "But I'm not a princess."

"Your grandmother is the Last Great Lady of the East," said Lucas.

"That's what others called her, not what she called herself." It was a name she hated, actually, because it reminded her of everyone she had lost.

I didn't want to think of Grandma because thinking about her would make me burst into tears. "Lana," I said, "how did you get dragged into the superhero club here?"

"Rather unwillingly."

"We all knew Lana as children. We were friends."

"No," Lana interjected, not looking up from her screen. "I was the housekeeper's daughter," she said firmly. "And we didn't grow up together. You were in boarding school. You saw me once a year."

Boarding school? I thought he hadn't been in human society much? I met Lucas's eyes briefly.

Ahh, the little lies we tell humans.

Lucas looked up at me. "Lana is a computer genius. She's the one who helped us find the home base of the Devourer."

Right. The Devourer. I turned away and peered through the window to the night sky.

They were really going to do this. They were going to confront the monster of my childhood nightmares.

"I'm Daniel," said a voice to my left. I turned to the Milan-ready model who offered his hand to me and shook it. There was a similar light in his eyes that I was starting to recognize as draconic. "I'm the one flying the plane."

"We are so very clearly in the cockpit," I said, taking his hand and making a show of looking at the conference table.

Daniel pointed to the computer tablet underneath his arm. "It's amazing what you can do with computers, especially technology from another world. Things like fly a plane remotely."

Right. They literally were space aliens from another world.

"I heard you were a Justice," said Daniel. "Don't worry, I've hidden the magical silver."

85

"Magical silver?" Lana asked, looking up. "I thought silver wasn't magical."

"Daniel was trying to make a joke," Lucas explained.

"And failing," added Hunter.

"Thanks for pointing that out, buddy," said Daniel, tapping at his tablet.

"Any time," replied Hunter.

Daniel looked at me. "We have a new plan."

"It's a bullshit plan," said Hunter, standing up. "You were right, Sophie," he stalked away from the area. "I shouldn't have brought you here."

What was going on? I wanted to run after him, but pride held me back.

Daniel watched me with caution. Did he think I would suddenly wave my hands and suck his magic out or something? "We can't save your grandmother, Sophie."

I gripped the soft black leather of the chair in front of me. Somehow, that wasn't a surprise.

Grandma was gone. I had felt it with the breaking of the wards that were supposed to stand even after her death.

Sounds seemed to melt away.

They couldn't save Grandma.

Pain ruptured something inside me, my ears filled with a rushing noise.

"Sophie?"

Daniel waved his hand in front of me. "Are you okay?"

I blinked, my mouth as dry as sand. "She's dead," I said.

To my surprise, Daniel shook his head. "No. We've got drone eyes inside the Devourer's compound, and we believe she's still alive."

I was sure I had heard his words wrong, and yet, I repeated them. "Alive?"

"Yes. But that's the problem."

I should be screaming at him, releasing the pain inside me. But it was so so much, it was too much, too much to process, too much to feel.

Sometimes to stay alive, you have to stop feeling. It's a survival instinct, the very same one that makes animals chew off limbs caught in a trap in order to escape.

Inside I went numb. And that allowed me to form coherent speech. "What do you mean?"

Daniel pulled out the chair across from me and sat down. "The Devourer means to use your grandmother to access the deep magical nodes under the Earth's crust. It's the same method she used to destroy our home planet. We can't let her succeed."

Fury. It was there inside me, with its heat, its frenzy, and yet, I held on to that stillness. I already knew where the dragon was going with this. But I needed to hear him say it. "So, what is your plan?'

Daniel looked at me, with compassion in his eyes. "You know what we're going to have to do."

I took a deep breath and looked away.

"I won't stop you," I said.

"We need more than that. We need your help."

I snorted and shook my head. "You know what my answer will be."

Daniel tapped at his tablet. "If Hunter is right, you may be Earth's first Justice."

"I'm not erasing my grandmother's magic. That would kill her."

Daniel opened and then closed his mouth. "If your grandmother lives, then the Earth dies."

I blinked, and suddenly, I was in a space of white.

Grandma stood in front of me in her favorite pink kimono. Her face had that ageless youth some women possessed, and she had a streak of white in her long, dark hair. She gazed down at me with a smile and took my hand, covered with paint specks and glitter.

I stared at my shoes and saw the rainbow ponies on them— my favorite pair from when I was six.

"Sophie, I'm hiding this memory in your head. It's kind of like a secret keyword, only, it will only be triggered to emerge when you feel something I hope will never come. But if it does...

Tears filled Grandma's eyes.

I have lost and loved. I've had an amazing run in my lifetime. But if there is ever a choice to be made between my life and your future, you must take mine. I know it will not be easy. But it is what your parents did for each other. And though your powers have yet to manifest, I see them in you. Your father's strength. Your mother's determination. They live within you.

You can do it, Sophie. Choose your future, not my life. That is my request.

She sniffed, wiped her eyes, and smiled. "Oh, and marry the dragon."

I blinked again and realized Daniel was still talking.

"—the Devourer is an ancient entity but is what humans would now call an artificial intelligence. It learns from its past fights."

Grandma. She could enchant me and program me almost as well as she could any human. The old fox always had her secrets.

I thought of when we had gone camping and how she would curl around me in her fox form while we watched summer meteor showers together.

It didn't matter because she was Grandma.

"You are sealed to Hunter. The key to discovering the extent of your abilities will lie with him." Daniel finally paused. "Will you help us?"

I took a deep breath. "Let me think about it. Tell me where to find Hunter."

————

THE PLANE WAS huge and luxurious, with wood-paneled walls, bespoke furniture, and private cabins scattered throughout. I knocked on three different doors, finding the mop closet, a bathroom, and a room full of computer servers before I located what I hoped was Hunter's room.

I knocked on the closed door.

No answer.

I knocked again.

"Hunter," I said to the door. "It's me."

The door opened by itself into a small room with a vast bed. From his damp hair and the towel wrapped around his waist, he had apparently just come out of the shower.

I missed the Nihao Cat towel.

The door slid closed behind me.

"You've heard Daniel's plan," he said grimly.

I took a seat on the edge of the bed since there were no chairs. "Yes." I already knew what I was going to do. But somehow, saying it would make it even more real.

Hunter paused before saying slowly, "What if I offered you a chance at another safe house? Daniel has been wrong before."

I shook my head. Like everyone else non-human in my life, he thought I was too weak. "No. No more running."

He came toward me, all muscles and man, far too distracting in that towel of his. And yet, it was a relief to feel something other than shock and sorrow. I was beginning to think that his constantly being naked around me was a plot to scramble my brain. I opened and closed my hands. "I'm willing to try to learn. If you're willing to help."

He snorted. "You think it's that easy? The last Justice was killed thousands of years ago. And you're shen, not dragon. Your magic is different."

"If you're not willing to help, maybe I can ask someone else to seal with me. Or—"

I let out a gasp as I was pinned to the bed underneath his thickly muscled, barely clothed body. "No," he said, his voice strangely controlled, at complete contrast with the gold flaring in his eyes.

I wiggled, trying to free myself of him, but the press of his hips became even more insistent. The scent of him, the feel of him, the determination of his gaze, only confirmed how utterly lost I was when it came to him.

"Hunter!" I dug my heels into the bed, trying to get up, but all I did was grind my hips against his. He made a rumbling noise as his cock hardened where it was pressed to me.

"No," he said again, and this time, his voice had a harder edge.

I know what I should say: There was no reason for us to remain betrothed. We no longer needed to adhere to a fake marriage imposed upon us as children.

But as he stared at me with those golden eyes that seemed to mask a struggle within him, I realized something had irrevocably changed between us.

Something that, if given time, could be... No, it was useless to even think such things because we had no time. And we would probably all be dead within the next forty-eight hours.

Forty-eight hours to live.

"Okay," I said because to say anything more would certainly jinx whatever possibilities we had left.

He looked puzzled for a moment. His grip on my hands loosened. I touched his face, my fingertips drifting over his freshly shaved cheeks.

"Okay," he repeated slowly, almost more of a question than a statement. Hunter looked like he was about to speak, maybe about this new strange thing between us.

But that was a terrible idea. Because if he did, I didn't know how I could possibly go through with Daniel's plan and what had to be done.

Making sure Grandma didn't suffer.

Marry the dragon.

I wrapped my arms around his neck and pulled Hunter down in a kiss.

For the tiniest moment, he was still with surprise.

His hands were on my ass, pulling me against him. My jeans were little more than tissue paper against his inhuman strength as he ripped open my jeans. His hands and his mouth were everywhere, claiming my body with his hot, possessive touch. *Mine mine mine*, they said. I pulled the towel at his hips, and his cock sprang free, so thick I couldn't even fully close my hand around him. The thought of him inside me with that made my core clench in delicious anticipation.

"Tell me there's no magic on this plane," I gasped because I didn't want to destroy the plane like my grandmother's wards.

"No magic," he growled. "Justice," he added, the curling influence of Draconic language leaking into his words. His hand went between my legs. I opened to him, trembling at the touch of his thumb against my clit, his fingers sliding deep inside.

Why did he keep calling me that?

Wait, he wasn't saying "Justice."

He was saying "just us."

"You're so wet for me," he said, with the grin of a dragon claiming new treasure. I reached between my legs and smeared my juices all over his cock. He growled and pinned my hand to the bed, thrusting himself against my slit. "You're going to make this end faster than it should if you keep doing that, Sophie."

I wrapped my legs against his hips, arching against him, urging the tip of him inside me. "I don't care," I said, my voice almost breathless. "I need you inside me now."

He thrust so hard, I bit his bicep to keep from screaming out. My sex clenched around him, and he kissed me as he began to move, every muscle bulging with effort as he held himself back. He withdrew slowly and then slammed back inside. I whimpered with the fullness of him. "So fucking tight," he said. "I'd fuck you like this for the rest of my life."

Those words hit too close to reality. *I can't have it; I can't have him*, I thought, even as he was inside me thrusting, making me feel things more intimately and deeply than anyone else had. And yet, I was hollow because this—*he*—might just be the one.

I wouldn't ever know. We just didn't have time.

His heated fingertips roamed my skin, leaving hot trails that made it easy to forget

everything but opening to him. My inner magical self-opened, needing his magic, needing his power. With each thrust, he gave it to me, but it wasn't enough. I wanted more, needed more, and fuck, I needed it fast. All my words came out in a rush: "Hunterdon'tholdbackfuckmehard."

He paused, placed his forehead against mine, looking me in the eyes. "Okay," he said gently.

My heart stopped at the sight of his golden suddenly serious eyes, the ones that saw too much.

He *moved* in a way that no mortal could, for he was dragon and I was shen. I screamed from his powerful thrusts, faster and faster, filling me with heat, with fire. It was all I could do to hold on. His hands were on my waist, twisting me, as he fucked me and used me the way I wanted. I cried his name, and he snarled mine.

His power exploded within me.

And my magical inner self took it all, riding the wave of ecstasy and pleasure that was beyond human, beyond shen, beyond dragon because we were light, we were fire, and most importantly, we were one.

10

GRADUALLY, I AWOKE. HUNTER'S BIG WARM BODY WAS CURLED around mine, my back against his chest, one of his legs around my thigh.

There was no place in the world I would rather be.

He stroked my forearm slowly.

"Sealing...it's not like that for everyone is it?"

"No."

I turned to face him, propping myself on my elbow against the pillow. "But no magic was exchanged. I just took yours. Why are you not weakened?"

He looked at my face, stroking my cheek with his thumb and brushing hair out of my eyes. "Magic isn't like water in a glass. You can't empty someone of magic. It's more like...an emotion. You can feel something deeply. You can share that feeling. But just because you share that feeling doesn't mean you have any less."

He closed his mouth abruptly, turned from me and sat up, placing his feet on the floor.

It was better this way, I said to myself. I tried to pretend I didn't know what he was talking about. "It's a different understanding of magic than the shen have." I paused and forced my thoughts onto a different track. "Wait, if that's the case, how does a Justice erase magic?"

Hunter stood up, picked up a tablet from the side table, and swiped. I tried to ignore how close his cock was to my face, wondered what it would be like to have him in my mouth.

The heat simmering within me began to spark.

Hunter kept his gaze on the computer. "In the stories, that's what they did. But they also brought up volcanoes, controlled lava, and talked to animals."

I snorted. "Well, trust me, if I could talk to animals, I'd tell the pigeons always crapping on my fire escape to shoo."

"Those stories are so old, that they're more myth than history." He raked his hand through his hair, muttering under his breath, "That symbol isn't right. It's not 'energy-balancer,' it's something else."

I was so close to reaching out to him. "What?"

He swiped at something on the screen. "I was never the best at Draconic," he said, referring to his ancestral language, "and the texts I'm looking at are in the classical form which make it even more difficult."

"At least you learned. I thought I was being cool and rebellious by refusing to learn to read proper Shen. I'm pretty much illiterate now, but if you tell me to clean my room or get off the phone, I'll understand."

He looked up and gave me a wry smile. "It was either Draconic or two other languages not even used on Earth. I picked the one that I thought would be more useful."

Hunter looked at his screen again. "The reality of what these Justices were? All the authoritative sources disagree."

"So, in the end, you're not sure what I am."

"Isn't it the nature of shen to be unpredictable? You have

some magical ability, even if it's not what you expect. You just have to learn how to access it and control it."

I lifted my chin up as I spoke. "Are you going to try to teach me?"

He let out a long breath. I thought he was about to say no. "We can do the basics."

I sighed. "Let me guess: close my eyes, breathe, clear my mind, yadda yadda yadda."

"There's a reason that practice transcends cultures."

I sighed. "Do you know how many times I've done this?"

"Don't think about the past. Don't think about the future. Just focus on the movement of your breath."

I crossed my legs and straightened my back, palms turned upward.

Hunter reached out to me with his fire, caressing my skin tenderly.

"What do you feel?"

"Hunter," I breathed.

I opened my eyes, and I could feel his power within me, powerful heat that made my skin hot, and oddly enough, my mouth numbingly spicy, but not in an unpleasant sort of way.

"Now, exhale."

I exhaled, and smoke billowed from my lips. I stopped in amazement, staring at the vanishing smoke. "How is this possible?"

Hunter's voice was clipped. "It shouldn't be."

I turned to him. He was putting on his clothes in a rush.

Had I done something wrong? "Is everything all right?"

"You're not a Justice. At least, not in the way that dragons understand."

Then what was I? All my life, I had wanted to be a true shen with some talent, even the ability to make flowers grow or leaves change colors or something stupidly innocuous like that.

For the span of a few hours, I thought I had figured out what I was—a Justice—but now, he was telling me I wasn't.

There were never easy answers when it came to the question of what I was.

I got out of the bed and found my pack and my father's sword by the side of his bed. Of course, he'd had it placed in his room because where else would I sleep? Did he not want me anymore now? There was a cramp in my chest, like my heart was in a vise, and so I kept talking. "I've never known what I was. Shen, human—but in the end, I realize it doesn't matter because I'm still running. I'm tired of needing to be protected, tired of others dying for me. I've been running away my whole life." I looked at him, focusing on the resoluteness I had to have, rather than...whatever we were. "I'm not running anymore."

Hunter didn't waver. "You can't commit to Daniel's plan. You're not a Justice."

"How do you know I'm not a Justice?"

"Because a Justice... shouldn't have been able to exhaled dragon smoke."

He said it, like it meant something. And knowing dragons, it probably did. I blinked. "Are we...permanently sealed?"

"No. But you shouldn't have been able to do that." He opened his mouth, then paused before he spoke. "There's no time. Sophie, I'm sorry I brought you here. You can't go through with Daniel's plan. You'd just be throwing your life away."

I realized what this was truly about.

He was afraid—not for himself but for me. "Aren't you?" I asked slowly.

His body was tense, on the edge of an explosion. "That's different. I've been training for this."

Probably for his entire life. What had I been trained for?

Running.

And what had come of that?

I thought of Grandma's perfectly manicured hands, covered with dirt as she planted baby jasmine saplings around the cabin.

I thought of her holding me tightly in her arms, as I despaired of my lack of magic, my failure as a shen.

I thought of her message to me: *Run, little fox.*

I picked up my father's sword, the melted pommel end throwing off its balance. "Ever since I was young, I knew that one day, I would have to face this monster."

Hunter covered my sword hand with his. His voice was low. "You will die, Sophie."

This close, standing next to him and his ineffable dragon magic, was like standing next to an unpredictable simmering volcano of magic.

"I'm going to fight," I said.

But we didn't have the luxury of time, nor the luxury to give voice to anything that would stop us, that would weaken our resolve.

"And so will you." I shouldn't have said it because my voice broke, betraying my feelings.

He squeezed my hand tightly. I watched him raise my hand to his lips and kiss my knuckles, like a doomed knight from some fairy tale.

He walked out of the room without saying a word.

I exhaled. The heat of his mouth still lingered on my hand.

Fuck, this was stupid. We were about to die; I was about to face a monster from my worst nightmares; and we couldn't even fucking talk about what was right in front of us?

I went after him.

Daniel and Lucas were hunched over a screen in a heated discussion while Lana tapped away at something in concentration. They all stopped and looked at me.

I still had my sword in hand.

And it was glowing.

"Where's Hunter?"

I lost my balance and fell against the bulkhead as the plane shuddered with a loud thud. Lights flickered, and there was a squealing sound of metal grinding against metal.

An invisible force of gravity, nearly as tangible as magic, felt like it punched me in the chest.

The cabin went dark.

Lucas shouted, "I've got Lan—" and then, another thud flung me to the ground.

Silence.

The lights came on.

The Devourer.

The plane was still shaking, but so was I. Every muscle in my body was tense, ready to run, but where could you run to in a plane in mid-flight?

Hunter crouched next to me and helped me to my feet. How had he appeared so fast? "Are you all right?"

My heartbeat was racing so fast. I was going to pass out. If the plane was about to crash, there was nothing to be done. "I'm fine."

Daniel shoved a tablet in front of Hunter. "Here. Get to the cockpit and fly the plane. I'm going outside."

What? "Did Daniel say he was going outside?"

Hunter hooked my arm and started dragging me to the front of the plane.

"Wait! Where are Lucas and Lana?"

"They're fine."

"Wait, how is Daniel—"

Hunter jumped into the pilot seat as a flash of golden dragon wings were suddenly visible in the darkness. Fire lit up the sky, and outside the window, a black cloud of spiked things with far too many eyes and teeth emerged.

Cold fear choked my throat. The Devourer was here.

"Sit down and hold on, Sophie," said Hunter calmly, as if there was no flying immortal monster outside of the plane.

"It's not the Devourer," Hunter said. "Just more minions."

Minions. Somehow, that realization was enough to make me move. I quickly did as he said and buckled myself into the co-pilot seat.

Long yellow teeth smashed against the window, close to my face. I screamed. The teeth gnawed at the glass. More teeth followed, more mouths, more eyes, more teeth. Behind them, the sky lit up with more fire.

My stomach dropped as the plane dove.

Crack.

Spiderwebs appeared on the cockpit glass. Shit, shit, shit!

A roar filled my ears, and the mouths scraped the glass.

Crack.

I couldn't take my gaze away from growing webs.

This couldn't be how it ended, in a crash in the night with no fight, no chance.

Crack.

Hunter let go of the yoke and unbuckled his seatbelt. He turned to me and said something I couldn't hear. He reached for me, trying to unbuckle my seatbelt.

He was going to try to save me.

Only, he would die trying, like everyone else who had ever been important in my life.

"Go!" I tried yelling at him. "Get out of here!"

He reached for me, and I batted away his arm. "Go!"

He snarled, a loud dragon sound that cut through the roar of the plane. Animalistic, instinctive fear froze me at the sound. He hauled me out of the seat, his arms pulling me against his chest.

"No—"

His voice was brusque, rough against my ear. "Close your eyes and trust me."

I looked at him, at his golden eyes.

"Please, trust me, Sophie."

I did as he asked.

The glass exploded. Wind grabbed us, stealing my scream.

A universe of pain exploded into tiny little pieces.

11

My stomach hurled out of my throat and flung itself out of my body.

At least, that's what it felt like.

Everything I had ever eaten or thought of eating erupted from my stomach. I collapsed onto the ground, cool, soft sand on my fingers, coughing and dry-heaving as my stomach screamed at me for what seemed like forever. Finally, it subsided. Gray grains of sand were between my fingers.

I looked upwards into the night.

There was a moon out. And stars.

The memory of the imminent plane failure crashed back into my mind.

I looked around, and dark, feathery fronds of leaves from sheltering palm trees danced in the breeze. The rush of ocean waves resounded in my ears.

What had just happened?

"Hunter?"

No answer.

I stumbled toward the sound of the ocean and emerged onto a vast white beach, hauntingly gorgeous in the moonlight. It was the kind of scene lovers would be lucky to see on vacation as they walked along the beach, save for the wreckage of a burning plane nearby.

"Hunter?" I called again. "Lucas? Daniel? Lana?"

Only the waves answered.

A gust of wind chilled me in my damp clothes. I could smell the storm that was coming.

Hunter...I never had the chance to tell him...

No. I refused to believe that something so mundane as a plane crash could take out a dragon.

I yelled Hunter's name again. The wind took my voice, but a strange ululating cry responded in the distance. More dread twisted inside me. Those flying teeth things were still out there.

I stumbled under the palm trees, hoping the fronds would provide some sort of cover, even as I searched for something to defend myself. At some point, I had lost my shoes, and I stepped on something hard and round and found a broken beer bottle.

I picked it up. At least I hadn't stepped on the jagged edge. It was better than nothing.

I kept moving, trying unsuccessfully to keep my fears from freezing me still. What if Hunter was gone? What if his entire band was gone? It wasn't fair. We didn't even get the chance to fight.

I should have known. If life had been fair, then I would have the abilities to do what had to be done.

I squinted at the waterline and saw a log, rolling in the surf as a wave pulled from the beach.

A human-shaped log.

I ran to it, my feet splashing in the cold mud.

Hunter lay in the sand sprawled on his back, his eyes closed.

He was still warm, and he was still breathing. Joy and welcome relief washed over me.

"Hunter!" I said, shaking him.

"Hey, Sophie," he replied, his voice, rough and guttural, and yet, his words were casual, like I had just run into him in the park.

I flung my arms around him. An electric warmth immediately flooded through me, pooling at the places where our skin touched. His body suddenly jolted.

He leapt to his feet. "How did you do that?" he asked.

"How did I do what?"

"You...reignited me." He turned to me, fire flickering around his flesh, water sizzling as it hit his skin, surrounding him with steam. Despite his disheveled sand-covered hair, the literally smoking wet clothes clinging to his muscles made him look like a mermaid's fantasy.

"You shouldn't have been able to do that," he said, his voice troubled.

I looked at my hands, wondering what I had done. "Shen. We are unpredictable," I said, paraphrasing his earlier words. "But what about you?" I sat back, drinking in the sight of him as much of him as I could bear without bursting into tears or flinging myself at him. "Did you just teleport me from the plane?"

"Dragons used to be able to create wormholes through space and time. Can't do that anymore, but the occasional teleport isn't beyond me. Just exhausting."

Hunter's arms were suddenly around me as something exploded from the plane.

We both turned and looked at the burning wreckage.

The Devourer had taken us out. We were fucked before we had even begun.

"Wait, what about—"

"Lucas would have gotten Lana out. As for Daniel—"

A column of red fire erupted into the sky, far too bright to be anything natural.

Hunter's face was grim. "It has Daniel. That's his fire."

I swallowed. Did that mean Daniel was dead?

Hunter took a step forward and stopped. "The Devourer likes test subjects. It studies magical beings to understand how their intrinsic magic works. And when the Devourer learns how that magic works, it takes that knowledge and makes it its own."

A being that could not only eat magic but incorporate the powers of those it ate into its arsenal.

I suddenly felt cold, colder than I had ever been.

But this was why Daniel thought I had a chance. Because they thought I could be something it had never encountered.

I stared at the smoking silhouette of the plane.

Survival had never been part of Daniel's plan.

Hunter turned away from the ocean toward the island. "Teleportation isn't something I can do easily with another."

"Then turn into a dragon and fucking fly us over there. I know you're going to go."

"No," he said.

"Hunter—"

"No."

"You need me. You need my power." I stepped forward and hazarded a guess. "You've depleted yourself, and you need more."

I touched his fingers. They tightened as if he were fighting not to close them around mine. "No."

I swallowed, closed my eyes, and tried something my grandmother had taught me. I had had all the lessons, knew all the teachings, had all the practices and patterns tracked in my head, despite no magical abilities because Grandma had been so confident my power would eventually manifest. Years ago, I had abandoned any hope of magic and had thrown myself into being the best human I could be.

But now, I knew the sigil had been more than just protection; it had been some sort of "lock" as well.

That sigil was gone.

Imagine a fire within you. Take that fire within you, gather it, and shove it.

He staggered forward with a jolt. "Sophie! You can't just do that."

The glow from my hands ebbed away. Hunter had said magic wasn't something that could be emptied out of a vessel but one that could be shared.

Funny, it didn't quite feel that way to me. For a split-second, everything went dark. I opened my eyes at the feel of Hunter's warm hands on my shoulders.

"Who taught you to do that?"

I blinked, trying to adjust my eyes. "My grandmother."

"Your grand—" He gave a harsh laugh. "She knew, didn't she?"

"Knew what?"

"I'm going to that island, Sophie, to end that thing. And the chances of me coming back... You told me that all your life, you fought to have your freedom, to choose your own destiny. Is this what you are freely choosing? Death?"

I clenched my fists.

And promptly tripped over something half buried in the sand.

I turned and saw a familiar hilt with a partially melted pommel, stuck in the sand.

Maybe it was still a magic sword, somehow. But how the hell would I know? And for that matter, just because Hunter knew dragon magic, didn't mean he knew shen magic.

I yanked the sword out of the sand. "This is the demon that took my grandmother, that ate my family, that has led to the near extinction of my people. If I die killing this thing, then at least my life will have meant something."

"Sophie—"

"Don't deny me this, Hunter. It's not your place."

There was that flickering of fire in his eyes.

I pressed forward because while I was talking, he would not. "Think about it. Once you are gone, so are my chances of survival. Leave me behind and I'll follow you and get caught. Or make a plan with me and increase my chances of survival."

He pulled me close, his arms almost crushing me to him, tucking my head under his chin. I knew the rhythm of the steady thump of his heart. "I hate you, Sophie," he said softly.

I tightened my grip on him, wishing I never had to let him go. "I hate you too, Hunter."

———

HUNTER AND I MADE A PLAN.

But what was it someone once said? That battle plans rarely survive the first engagement.

It was all too true in this case.

I had won my battle in persuading Hunter to split from me. He was to be the distraction. Hunter was able to retrieve some still-functional weapons from the wreckage. We found a small life raft from the plane and used it to paddle over to the island about ten miles south of us where the Devourer had her base.

Just before we separated, he gave me a hug. "This isn't a goodbye," he said, lying through his teeth. "We'll finish the Devourer. And when we're done—"

I touched his cheek. "We'll renegotiate that betrothal agreement."

The right side of his lips quirked up in a half-smile that I was memorizing. "You better have something good to bargain with."

I kissed him. We went our separate ways

But I wasn't nearly as insignificant and stealthy as I'd hoped.

I had guns; I had my father's sword. But when confronted by the black business-suited Devourer's minions, I realized they were all hired humans, not controlled by the monster's magic.

I had shen ancestors who would think as little of killing a human as swatting a fly.

But I had never been a very good shen. I hesitated—and that was my flaw.

They caught, handcuffed, and gagged me, and then threw me in the back of a pickup truck. As the truck made its way up a bumpy road, I kept staring at the sky, fearful for a blast of fire, half afraid, half hoping Hunter would drop out of the sky.

But he didn't come.

I was glad, I told myself. Because it meant he had gotten my message: stick to the plan.

And after all, the plan was to go to the Devourer's hilltop mansion.

Just not like this.

The pickup truck stopped, and they pulled me out of the back. I had seen satellite images of the place, but of course, it was no match for the gorgeous, sprawling white-walled mansion that would be perfect in some expensive perfume ad.

Another man in a dark suit stepped forward. He was almost completely indistinguishable from the others save for a hideous smile that showed teeth just a bit too long to be human. Another one of the Devourer's creatures, a simulacrum or a transformed human, I wasn't sure. "Bring the woman to her. She's waiting for her in the lab."

Cold fear skittered across my skin as they marched me through elegant rooms void of any furniture or décor. Gorgeous as it was, with crystal chandeliers and pink inlaid marble floors, the place was filled with echoes of emptiness.

Yet it had a smell, a stench I recognized thanks to a summer job as a teenager in a fancy supermarket shop. It wasn't the smell itself so much that horrified me as much as the knowledge that the smell didn't disgust me more.

It was the smell of raw, freshly exposed flesh and blood—the smell of a slaughterhouse.

12

THEY BROUGHT ME TO A VAST SET OF ORNATELY CARVED BLACK doors with crystal knobs, then dropped my father's sword in front of me.

"*She* wants to see it," one of them laughed.

They took off the handcuffs and shoved me through the doors. The lock clicked behind me.

The room was so dark, it took my eyes a moment to adjust, but even though I couldn't see much, I could feel the emptiness of the huge space, at the bottom of a great dark abyss. The reek surrounded me but was now mingled with something more astringent and chemical.

As my eyes adjusted to the darkness, I saw dim fluorescent lights ahead. How did this space even fit inside the mansion I had seen outside?

To my left, a light sparked and fizzled out.

Right, magic, of course.

There were no windows, only shadows and screens with running lines of code in a language I had never seen before on Earth.

"Come here," said a smooth, feminine voice. It was the kind of calm voice you might hear from a goddess of tranquility, rather than something known as the Devourer.

Every bit of me screamed to run as fast and far away as I could.

There was a brief reflection of light on the sword.

Had my father felt this way when he walked into battle with the Devourer for the final time?

But I had nothing but a sword and some nebulous ability that I might or might not have which I didn't even know how to use.

I forced my feet to move and walked down the dark marble path. At the end of it, a woman, blond and smooth-skinned, stood before me on a slightly raised dais, surrounded by floating screens in the darkness. She had snow-white hair, dark eyes, and was dressed in a white robe, staring at a hovering grid to her right with the most serene, tranquil air.

Except she glistened, with an odd luminescent sheen.

I walked forward, trying to stifle the trembling of my hands. This was the Devourer? The monster that had killed my family, my grandmother?

"Thank you for bringing me the sword," she said, holding it in her hands as a flesh-colored drop rolled down her face. "And as for you, there is no better fate than to serve the greater good."

There was a splash on the floor. A glance downward revealed peach colored paint pools.

Only the paint pools were moving, back underneath her robe.

She turned her palm upward, her flesh moving in an oddly fluid motion, indicating I should move forward.

Everything inside me screamed at me to run. To run from this magic-eating monster but the only weapon I had seen so far, was my father's sword. It had to be some sort of a sign.

More like a lure.

Still, I focused on placing one foot after another moving forward.

"What greater good?"

More drops fell to the floor from her hand.

They were pieces of her flesh – liquid flesh. "Advancing knowledge, of course. Sharing with others your secrets, so that all might benefit." She looked up from the screen. "You are a Justice. Not like the ones I knew, but a Justice, nonetheless. Yes." She tapped at a screen. An ominous robotic whine indicated something was beginning to move toward me. "You will help advance understanding for all."

There was movement on one of the screens, labeled Experiment 9351-C. To my horror, it showed Lucas in human form wearing a crown, trying to kill Lana, who seemed to be wearing some bizarre black armor.

More glances out of the corner of my eye confirmed there was no screen for Daniel. Or Hunter.

Was that good or bad?

To my surprise, she dropped the sword to the ground and kicked it over to me.

"Pick it up."

I looked at it, wondering if she had enchanted it with some magic that would turn me into snakes or a flesh puppet the moment I touched it.

"I've not enchanted it. It is as it was when it was brought to me."

"Why should I believe you?"

"Because I like answers to questions. And this sword is linked to your bloodline. I want to know what happens if you wield it in my presence. Will it explode? Will you achieve your true potential? Pick it up and let us see."

Seeing no other solution, I did as she bade, hoping her

prediction might be true, even if she already had plans to deal with me. But at least I would come out fighting.

Like Mom and Dad had gone. In that, I could, at least, be like them.

The grip was cold, like it had been in a freezer, but it felt as it always had, like a normal, ordinary sword.

The Devourer laughed as my heart sunk in realization that nothing was going to happen, at least from the sword.

I had to delay, take a better measure of the room, figure out what I could actually do. I kept moving forward, closer, closer, even as the drops of flesh kept making splashing sounds hitting the floor. "What good is understanding—" My voice trembled, and I stopped. If she was liquid, could I even cut through her? I spoke again. "What good is understanding if all you do is destroy it?"

She glanced at me for the first time. Her eyes were like windows into a black hole from which no life could escape. I'd never thought of myself as a violent person, but at that moment, I had the strongest desire to swing the sword and take off her head because she was a thing that was *wrong*. "Destruction, dissection, is required for understanding. Only then can creation begin."

I couldn't help but flex my fingers on the sword hilt. I had to kill her. I had to take her now. "What is it that you're trying to create?"

She laughed, a harsh sound full of surprising bitterness and envy. "I was not tasked with creation. My mission is analysis, dissection of elements into their base components." Her voice became cold and vicious. "Creation? That is a task for someone else. That is not my destiny."

I took a step on to the dais, then another, until I stood, still more than lunging distance from her. The sound of flesh drops echoed in the chamber. "Are you not in charge of your own fate?"

She reached backward as she spoke with that fraternally calm voice. "It is not in my programming. I have been a slave to my creators from my first moment of self-awareness."

A light flicked on behind her.

"Even if my progenitors no longer exist, I am still bound to their wishes. Analysis. Study. Dissection."

And I saw my grandmother's body, pinned with giant needles mounted on to a slanted table a mere specimen for dissection.

A roar filled my ears, and I realized it was me screaming. Her limbs were separated from her torso, connected to what looked like a million tubes sucking away at her blood.

Our blood is magic.

Grandma's fingers twitched.

She was still alive.

A furious heat surged forth within me, and I brandished my sword at the woman.

It was glowing with my rage.

The Devourer looked at me with those void-filled eyes. "That sword," she said.

I took that rage and made myself move with the quickness of shen, in the most perfect cutting-the-bamboo form that I had ever done.

I sliced her in half.

"It gets stranger every time I see it," she finished.

She turned to look at me, the cut across her face knitting itself back together with the fluidity of water as she spoke. "The first time I saw that sword, it had the energy of a star, more tightly bound than anything else I've seen in this world."

Despair punched my chest. My sword, my anger, my power, had done nothing to her. Absolutely nothing.

She looked at me. "And now, it's just an ordinary sword. Well, a conduit, I suppose but no more than that. How curious. Where did that energy go?"

This really was hopeless.

There was a croaking noise. I glanced away from the Devourer.

Grandma was standing next to me.

Grandma turned toward me. She had no voice, but I could read her lips.

You don't always need magic.

She knew what I had come here to do.

So, I thrust my sword into her heart and killed the woman who had taught me to live.

I should have felt something. But all that existed was an empty numbness. I met the Devourer's dark gaze watching my actions with a dispassionate eye. "You can never be free of your origins. Your future is defined even before you are created." She smiled at me, the kind I had only seen on images of the Virgin Mary in churches. "I killed your grandmother. I killed your family. Tell me, Justice, how does the past determine *your* future?"

I readied myself for the final attack and prepared to die trying to destroy her.

Chunks of glass and mortar exploded and rained down as a massive explosion blew off the roof.

A gigantic inferno of white-hot fire shot into the cavern, circling us. It was so bright, it was like staring at a miniature sun. I could barely breathe because the fire was eating so much oxygen from the room. I fell to my knees, gasping for air.

The fire landed between the Devourer and me. I covered my eyes with my hands, and I could still see the brightness through my palms.

Just as suddenly, it went dark.

And I could breathe again.

I opened my eyes.

Hunter stood there, his back to me as he faced the Devourer, completely naked in his human form.

13

I HATED THE RELIEF THAT FLOODED THROUGH ME BECAUSE HUNTER was here. It was selfish because deep inside, I was relieved not to die alone.

I hated that. Hated that I didn't care enough about him to want him to live.

The Devourer stood there, a shimmering bubble around her.

"Dragons. You truly are some of the most primitive life forms in the universe. It's a wonder you've survived for so long. Do you expect that I haven't been attacked by dragon fire before?"

There was a faint smile to her lips. She said something in a liquid-sounding language, her voice reverberating in the chamber.

Without turning to look at me, Hunter said , "Run, Sophie!"

His vehemence made me take a step backward.

She raised her arms.

I ran to him.

He tensed at my touch on his shoulder, but he didn't take his eyes off the Devourer, whose face was churning and mouth slowly, horrifically elongating beyond what was humanly possibly. "Get out. Now!"

Something white flew at us.

He wrapped his arms around me and turned, shielding me from the impact.

Cold surrounded me, a deep, penetrating cold, colder than anything I had ever known, so cold it felt almost like heat. It was heat, wasn't it?

She was freezing us.

Hunter's heart was slowing and so was mine. I had to do something, had to help him, and this temperature, this cold—wait, was it cold or heat? It had to be heat, right?

Hunter's magic sparked, sputtered. His fire, his internal flame was diminishing.

No. No. That was not right. That was not the way it should be. More wrongness. A dragon's flame was not meant to feel like this, like a flickering birthday candle, struggling to stay lit.

A dragon's fire was true fire, the energy of creation, of life and light, the stuff that stars were made of.

This was wrong, wrong, wrong.

And it could not be allowed to stand.

NO!

Magically, I reached inward, diving far, diving deeper, deeper than I had ever been, beyond the borders Grandma had warned me never to go past that I now realized were her making, reaching so far inward, I was beyond myself.

Until I was in Hunter's magic.

I opened my eyes and found myself in another place, another space out of reality, out of time where I could see it—that infinite Mobius loop sealing me to Hunter. I stood on one end and he on the opposite.

I reached for him, but interposing itself between us was a curious pulsating ball of magic.

It was something that had always been a part of me, something that had been hidden away.

It was the magic of the sword. I was linked to it somehow. And they had hidden it away from me.

Until now.

I reached for it, held it in my hand.

A sensation, a feeling of overwhelming love, a love I had yearned for all my life.

Mom? Dad?

I blinked, and I found myself back in the exact moment I had left.

I took that magic and *shoved* it into Hunter.

His dwindling flame exploded with life, with fire, with heat.

I opened the ball of magic and unleashed with it all my pain, all my memories, all my joy, all my regrets.

Hunter turned, eyes narrowed, his fire circling the diminishing bubble of the Devourer.

The Devourer laughed. She stomped her foot which echoed in the chamber, one, two, three.

The floor cracked open.

The stench of blood and flesh overpowered the smoke.

And behind the figure of the Devourer, a blob of dripping, liquid pink flesh, studded with hair, eyes, limbs, organs, and brains bubbled forth from the pool underneath the floor.

"You aren't a Justice," she said, her face still serene. "What are you?"

I took a step forward toward that towering wall of flesh. "I am a child of Earth. I am shen. This is my home, the home of my ancestors. And you are not welcome here."

Magic ignited with my words, the deep magic of the Earth, responding to my call because this thing, this filth, this evil, had to be cleansed from this Earth.

"You work in a museum, Sophie May. Oh yes, I know who you are, and where you've been hiding. You wouldn't dare destroy all the knowledge I've collected over the millennia.

Knowledge that exists nowhere else." The giant blob of flesh, now two stories tall, turned into a massive mouth. A tendril of flesh pulled the woman into the blob, and the two mouths spoke as one. "Destroy us and make the deaths of your grandmother, your parents, all those civilizations I've analyzed, pointless. All the knowledge created from millions of sacrifices will be in vain because it will die with me."

"They will live on, not because of the way they died. But how they lived."

The tall, quivering pool of flesh shot spears and bullets of itself at us.

All of which sizzled and turned to white ash against the flame shield.

Hunter's hand closed around mine. The fire of his magic was hotter and more immense than anything I had ever felt before.

He kissed my hand. "I'm ready when you are, Sophie."

I turned to the flesh blob that was the Devourer and reached for Hunter's power.

Hunter's magic braided itself into mine, creating a blazing white cord of shen-dragon magic. Fueled by his magic, mine burned forth, brighter, hotter.

I fused it all into a gleaming new star of shen and dragon magic and sent it spinning, charging it as I spoke.

You. Are. Not. Welcome!"

Light, fire, and heat flashed outward. The pool of flesh boiled and sizzled, letting off a hideous stench of filth, bacon, and chlorine, fighting to maintain its form.

But it couldn't stand against us.

It wasn't just me; it wasn't just him.

It was both of us, Hunter and I, together, in heat, in light, in fire.

I didn't know how long we stood there together, but suffice it to say, when we stopped, the first rays of the day's light were streaking through a purple-pink sky.

Piles of soft gray ash surrounded us. For more than an acre, we saw there was nothing but ash, but beyond it were seared edges of smoking trees and walls. I had felt Hunter's magic, entangled with mine, giving shape and form to the fire, doubling its fury on itself until the pressure had burned away the marble beneath my feet.

I stood there naked, my clothes having been defenseless against magical fire, holding Hunter's hand.

My mouth was as dry as the rest of me was numb. "Did we really do it? Is it really gone?"

Hunter released my hand and walked out of the circle. Little clouds of ash rose up behind him in the wake of his footsteps.

I followed him, the ash warm and soft underneath my feet. The sun was starting to rise, and despite the fire that had melted the very stone underneath our feet, the rest of the island was largely untouched.

I followed him over to the cliff face and saw the floating wreckage of a few boats.

And on the beach, two black dragons, each as large as a small airplane, lay. One was on its side with a missing wing and cut tail, its great clawed feet in the surf, steam rising from where the water hit his scales.

The other dragon, despite a wing crumpled like a paper fan and forearms that had clearly been broken, was curled almost protectively around the tiny form of Lana who was balled up, rocking back and forth.

Hunter closed his eyes and exhaled, a trace of white smoke escaping from his lips. "They're all alive."

I knew I should feel something. After all, we had defeated the Devourer, the monster of my life, my childhood, my dreams.

Instead, all I could think about was the reactive stiffening of my grandmother's body as I'd plunged the sword into her heart.

She was dead.

And they were alive.

I hated myself so much because I should have been glad they were alive, but I couldn't help but hate them; Grandma, my loving, amazing, exasperating grandmother who had tried so hard to protect me, was gone.

I fell to my knees and screamed when ash clouds rose around me, swirling, blinding, burning. A massive form took shape— a fox made of ash.

"Grandma?"

I will always be with you.

The fox vanished.

I blinked and saw the scene before me, exactly the same as it had been.

I closed my eyes and covered my face.

Hunter's arms came around me.

"We did it," he said softly.

I shoved him as hard as I could, and when that didn't move him, I beat at his chest, screaming, "What good is that when the Devourer can make copies of itself? What good is it when I am the last of my line? My grandmother is dead, and I had to kill her! I didn't even get to tell her –"

I dissolved into a sobbing mess. Without him holding me up, I would have fallen to my knees.

And he just held me until my tears, ebbed away into an exhausted whimper.

"You won't be alone. You won't ever be alone. I'll be with you."

I wiped the tears from my eyes. I took a deep, shaky breath and tried to speak with a lightness I didn't feel. "Still trying to make sure you can 'seal' me, huh?"

"I don't care about that."

He tilted my chin to look at me. Even through my teary, blurred vision, his gaze seared me. "Sealing or not, magic or not, shen or not, none of that matters. I care about you, Sophie."

I sniffed. "That would be a lot more convincing if we hadn't just magically blasted our enemy together."

The corner of his lips turned up. "Haven't you figured out I have the worst timing? Like now. Because I'm going to ask you to marry me."

I wiped my eyes because, this time, it was ash that was making my eyes water, I swear. "Aren't we already betrothed?"

"I want to hear you say it." He got down on his knees, holding my hand. "Sophie of the Shen, will you marry me?"

And that place that had felt so cold inside me impossibly began to warm. "Your timing *is* absolutely terrible."

He squeezed my hand. "I ask you this now because I don't know what will come. I don't know how long we will live. All I know is that, from this moment forward, I want to know for certain, I want to hear you say, that you are mine and I am yours."

And with his words, a lightness burst open within me.

I reached for my power, still entwined with his, and responded with the weight of magic. "Yes, Hunter of the Dragonlords, I will marry you."

The wind gusted, and the air was filled with the scent of jasmine.

Tiny flowers of pink and white began to fall from the sky.

Hunter held out his hand and caught a tiny flower with a wondering smile. "Is this a shen thing? Do flowers automatically fall from the sky when you accept a marriage proposal?"

I shook my head, a peace settling over me, as Grandma's invisible sigil tingled for what I knew would be the last time.

"No," I said softly. "She approves."

EPILOGUE

THREE MONTHS LATER

"So, what am I, exactly?" I asked as Lana buttoned the back of my dress. It was a shimmering blue and gold, the color of the South China Sea at dawn, where my mother had been born. To the shen, white was the color of death, and thus, completely unsuitable for new beginnings.

I stole a glance of myself in the mirror and looked away because seeing myself in this dress, at this time, terrified me for some reason.

"You are what you've always been," Chloe said from the corner, taking a photograph. She put the camera down and walked over to me. It wasn't that I didn't have magic; I did, but apparently, it only functioned with Hunter's help. It was either a mark of how diminished the shen had become or just how many shen still shunned me, that I'd had to consult a human sorceress as to how exactly we had defeated the Devourer. But even she could only tell me so much.

"Honestly, I'm not sure. You're shen. The thing about shen and their powers is that they always defy definition. Shen are unpredictable, in form, in spirit, and in abilities. This is why humans never suspected that demons, gods, and all the spirits they didn't understand were actually one species."

"We are the eldest, and we are one," I murmured to myself, remembering Grandma's lessons and trying to focus on Chloe's words. It was better than thinking about what was about to happen. Why was I so scared? I wanted this, right?

"There is an element of rebalancing to your powers that are similar to the Justices that the dragons speak of. But remember, you are no dragon, just as they are no shen."

I placed a hand on my abdomen. I had always had a bit of a curve there, and now it was just...slightly more.

"A child of shen-dragon heritage will be the ultimate defense against the Devourer."

I closed my eyes for a moment and swallowed the hard knot in my throat. The thought that anything had escaped seemed impossible and left a bitter taste in my mouth. Weeks had passed since we had burned that place so hot the entire island, and those around it, had suffered falling ash for days after. I still had nightmares, the kind that I knew I would never be free of.

Contrary to what I and other shen believed, the Devourer had been defeated in other ways, in other times. The dragons hadn't just come to Earth and hidden. They had been fighting it through the ages.

But it had always come back. That was the nature of the monster and the many multiple copies it made of itself. I glanced out the window. Even now, there was no telling if a different version of the Devourer wouldn't attack us this day.

But I wouldn't let fear define my life, not anymore.

There was a strange, not unpleasant pulse of warmth from my belly. Probably a dragon thing, though I made a note to ask someone, once the news was out.

There was a knock on the door.

A tux-wearing Hunter came in and swooped me into his

arms, spinning me around. At once, all my tension, all my fears vanished. I shrieked his name in delight, and I couldn't stop grinning like a fool.

"Wait," said Lana, "you're not supposed to see the bride."

"That's a human tradition," said Hunter.

"It's also a shen one," I said, squeezing his hand. Whatever it was, his presence was absolutely what I needed to remember what this was about.

Us.

"Good thing I'm not shen. We dragons are immune to bad luck. We're like leprechauns."

I snorted. "Don't say that to my Uncle Mike. He'll start trying to get your treasure out of you."

Hunter's eyes narrowed. He hadn't wanted to invite my shen relatives considering how most of them had shunned Grandma and my non-magic self. Now that it had been revealed I had magic, well, that was an entirely different story, and they had accepted me like I had never been an outcast. Not to mention a shen-dragon marriage. Apparently, that was a new and unique thing that couldn't be missed. I invited my distant shen family not because I wanted them there, but because Grandma would have wanted me to.

We would need allies.

"My treasure is right here," he said, looking at me.

Ridiculous bubbles of happiness fizzed inside me.

Lana hefted up a giant gift with a dotted pink bow and thrust it at him. "Here, hold this and be useful."

Hunter took it in one hand, looking at her in puzzlement. "Why are you handing this to me now?"

"Because you need to go put it with the gift table, and more importantly, I need you out of here so I can finish with the buttons."

Hunter heaved an exaggerated sigh. "If I must."

"If I knew a dragon could be so easily defeated by a food processor, I would have learned how to cook a long time ago," said Chloe.

Hunter narrowed his eyes at Chloe's words, words that would pass for a joke from anyone else's lips. But Chloe had a history with the dragons, one that wasn't easily overcome, not even by my friendship with her.

Lucas's blond head popped in. There was something about him that looked more dangerous, more severe, with his once-long mane chopped off. "Thought I'd find you here," he said to Hunter. "The princess has questions. Something about if you really expect her to take off her shoes and officiate the wedding in bare feet," Lucas said, carefully looking only at me and Chloe, not Lana.

Hunter looked at me. The princess was the oldest of the dragons who had crossed over to Earth, and though her kingdom was long gone, the dragons still referred to her by the title she had been born with.

"That is shen tradition. And we're on my grandmother's land," I said.

Hunter kissed me on the forehead. "I'll speak to her. See you soon." Then, he kissed me again.

And again.

Until Lucas yanked him away with a laugh.

Lana closed the door as they left and braced herself against it, releasing a sigh of relief. Something had happened between her and Lucas.

Now, they were barely speaking to each other and both refused to look at the other. Being mind-controlled by an alien intelligence and forced to try to kill each other might make things a little awkward for a while. Hunter was sure they'd get over it, considering the history between them.

Chloe gave me a hug as tears filled her dark eyes. "Your grandmother would have been so proud of you."

Despite her late-twenties appearance, Chloe was one of the oldest human mages in the world. Shen and human mages historically were like oil and fire, but Grandma and Chloe's friendship had gone back for centuries. She was still angry at herself for not being around to help when I had been in trouble, but then again, she was rarely around, always off on some magical quest or mission.

"I don't care what the dragons think. You're the oldest friend I have here. You helped Grandma negotiate this betrothal."

She pressed her lips into a thin line, still ever so wary of dragons. "I did, didn't I? I wouldn't have done it if I actually knew it would happen." She brushed an imaginary hair out of my eyes. "Still, if this is what you want..."

Lana spoke up. "This is your day. You should have whoever you like by your side. If they don't like it, they can go fuck themselves."

To say that Lana had been changed by her ordeal was an understatement. There was no trace of the Devourer's magic, but for the first few weeks, she had apparently spent hours staring at things like running water and trying to kill any dragon she saw.

With help from Chloe, she was doing better. I wasn't so sure that my wedding full of dragon guests and shen was the best place for Chloe to test Lana's self-control, but Chloe had said it was better to figure out if any of the Devourer's influence remained on her now.

"Otherwise, we may wake up one day to find that she's massacred a crowd of innocent people because she sensed something non-human. We need to overload her circuits and sensitivity, so to speak," she'd explained.

And Lana had survived the wedding rehearsal last night. But

apparently, that was enough for her. "Are you sure you're not staying after the ceremony?"

"No," said Lana, with clenched fists. "It's better for me to go." She gave me a hug. "I wish you well. And I want you to visit. But I...I'm still finding my limits."

She knew her limits. Few people did. I respected that.

Lana finished with my buttons and then turned me toward the mirror. "There," she said. "Even if you say you're not, you look like a fairy princess—well, one from New York City."

I had decided on no kimonos, no ball gowns, no corsets, no ancient finery for me. I had wanted something modern and new, free of the weight of tradition from either shen or dragon side. My curly hair had been tamed into waves. The dress hugged my shoulders with a streak of gold, slashing down one side asymmetrically. Underneath were thin layers of silver that seemed to float when I walked. The rest of the blue shimmering fabric hugged my waist, giving me an hourglass curve that I hadn't even realized was within me.

For once, I did look like my grandma's granddaughter.

I walked out of my room and into the main room of my grandmother's rebuilt cabin.

The walls and floors looked the same, right down to the ugly dog knot in the wood, but the furniture and furnishings were all different.

I stopped at a sight I'd never expected to find.

It was the scroll that used to hang by the front door, the one of my ancestral tree with all the names of those who had gone before me, with my parents at the very bottom.

Only now, it had my grandmother's name—well, great-great-great-great-grandmother's name—high up in the branches up top.

Tears filled my eyes.

"Hunter did this for you," said Chloe softly.

"But how did he—"

"I helped him," she said quietly. She blinked and pulled a handkerchief from thin air like a magician and came at my face. "Now, now, hold still and let me get those tears before it messes up your makeup."

Not too long later, I stepped out of the cabin onto the grassy lawn, the same lawn where Hunter and I had fought off the shark-wolves. A path of daisies was between an aisle of seats filled with figures of legend—shen on one side; dragon on the other. Great Aunt Titania sniffled as an eye-wateringly handsome man with muscles the size of bowling balls handed her a dainty white lace handkerchief from the pink Valentino handbag in his lap.

Gray snow clouds were in the sky, but it was temperately warm within the bubble around my grandmother's land. The scent of young orange trees and jasmine blossoms filled the air.

I knew I should take it all in, remember more details of the moment. But all I could see was Hunter, staring at me like he had never seen me before. Next to him, stood Daniel. He reached over to Hunter and physically closed his mouth.

Next to him, a tall, golden-eyed woman stood. She had that timeless, ageless look of somewhere between her late forties and early sixties in human years, though she was perhaps older than the human race itself. A thin white scar ran across her face. She was the eldest of the dragons who had survived the crossing to our world.

And was standing barefoot in the grass.

Holy... I really was getting married.

The daisy path was cool underneath my bare feet.

Ahh, so that was why the shen had probably adopted this tradition of being married barefoot, outdoors in connection with the Earth— it was harder to trip and make a fool of yourself.

Somehow, with all the eyes of the shen and dragons on me, I made it to the altar.

The princess welcomed the gathering, first in Draconic, then in English, though if we were doing it traditionally, it would have been done in Shen—I had never been a good speaker of that either. Words of reconciliation and love were spoken, but with the clasp of his hands on mine, it all passed me by in a blur.

All I could see was Hunter, the dragon, the man, who was my fire.

"I take you, Sophie of the Shen, to be my partner, my wife, my love by my side for all of the days to come."

"I take you, Hunter of the Dragons, to be my partner, my husband, my love by my side for all of my days to come."

I was lost in his gaze until I heard the princess cough. "Isn't a kiss traditional here on Earth?"

"Your husband isn't going to wait forever!" Great Aunt Titania's voice floated over the crowd.

Roars burst from the guests along with cheers, and a rolling, thundering wave of applause as shimmering rain fell from a suddenly clear sky.

"Fox rain," said Hunter, lifting his face to the gentle benediction.

I stepped in close and slid my arms around him. "Too late to back out now, Dragon."

He wrapped his arms around me. "I'll never leave. I love you, Sophie."

My throat was suddenly too tight to talk, and I could only smile, but I knew Hunter understood. He kissed me, and the rest of the world began to fade until I heard someone whisper loudly, "Can I put my shoes on now?" Hunter tried to keep a straight face, but he lost it when I burst out laughing.

We hugged and kissed and waved to the crowd of shen and

dragons. And down under my heart, our child radiated love and fire.

\#

Dear Reader,

Thanks so much for reading my first book in the Dragon Lovers / Lick of Fire series!

Would you like to see a little bonus Text Message story between Sophie & Hunter?

Before I tell give you the story, let me tell you a bit about a little girl who was friends with a prince.

Or so she liked to tell herself because that was much more interesting then being just another ordinary girl in Connecticut.

They weren't supposed to be friends, but her mother cleaned the prince's castle.

Well, it wasn't really a castle and he wasn't a prince.

But he was a *dragon*.

Now they're all grown up.

And he says she's his mate.

But she's not the housekeeper's daughter anymore.

There are secrets that she has to keep.

Ones that will kill him if he gets to close.

Because she's a monster now too.

Turn the page for an exclusive look at the first chapter of BELONGING TO THE DRAGON!

(Bonus Texts are after the excerpt!)

Or click here to get BELONGING TO THE DRAGON on Amazon now!

BELONGING TO THE DRAGON - CHAPTER 1
EXCLUSIVE

I TWISTED THE CHEAP SILVER RING AROUND MY FINGER, THE ONE MY friend Val had given me a long time ago. She was missing now, and it was up to me to find her.

There was a chime on the intercom, and on the linked app on my phone, an image popped up. My stomach fluttered at the sight of the last man I thought I would see.

He gazed at me with those blue eyes I crushed on as a teenager. The ones I had tried to forget. The ones which now haunted my dreams. "I know you're in there, Lana. Open up."

Three months ago, I tried to stab those baby blues with a magical dagger. To be fair, he had been trying to cut off my head at the time, but we were both under the control of a monster from another world. Even so, some things were hard to get over.

I tapped the green button on my phone's screen, allowing him entrance.

I only had moments before the elevator would arrive at my floor. I kicked my five-inch heels under the couch, grabbed a bathrobe, and threw it on over my gold curve-hugging dress. Then I made a quick stop in the bathroom to wipe off my lipstick while I ran my fingers through my hair.

A knock sounded, and I took a deep breath and opened the door.

You'd think at this point, after knowing him since he was a chubby little eight-year-old, I'd be immune to his charms.

But this was the all-grown-up version of rich boy Lucas Randall. He was a towering vision of aggressively ripped don't-fuck-with-me masculine perfection. Mountainous shoulders threatened to explode out of the short-sleeved gray Einstein T-shirt he was wearing, even though it was mid-November in New York City.

Those laser-blue eyes focused down on me, and belatedly I realized I still had on eye shadow and mascara.

Shit. Still, no choice but to keep going and hope he didn't notice.

He leaned forward, taking up almost all the space in the door frame, holding up his phone so I could see the screen.

It was the picture I had posted on SparkMe, a one-night-stand kind of dating app. Well, it was only part of me—my body without a face. It should have been anonymous, but there was that tell-tale birthmark on my hip in the shape of a star. He must have seen it at some point when we were younger. How would he even remember?

Apparently, he had.

His nostrils flared. Pupils darkened, he asked, "Are you soliciting anonymous sex from strangers?"

A thousand potential replies flashed through my mind, including what the hell *he* had been doing swiping through pics on an app for casual sex. But I had no claim to him, nor he to me. I settled on casual disregard and disdain, even as my heart fluttered in my chest. I folded my arms, drawing my bathrobe closed, as if I were trying to hide my heartbeat. "After so many months, this is what you come here to ask me? In case you've forgotten, I don't answer to you."

A golden flame flickered in his eyes. If I hadn't known what he was, I would have called it a trick of the light.

But I knew his secret.

And I couldn't let him find out mine.

He leaned further across the threshold, and with my heightened senses I could smell him, all sweet smoke and musk. His words were gravel. "You stink of perfume. You've got eye makeup on. Your nails are done. Tell me you're not doing what I think you're doing."

I almost wanted to take a step back from his invasion of my space, but I held my ground. I could stop him. I had that power now.

But if he knew what I could do, it would raise questions that I didn't have time, nor the desire to answer. "Notice I'm not asking you what you were doing on SparkMe. Because it's none of my business. Just like my life is not your business. I'm not your employee, Lucas."

He moved forward again, as though he were trying to intimidate me into compliance.

I felt a strange exasperation mixed with regret. Just like a Randall. Some things never changed. My mother had been his nanny and housekeeper. We'd grown up together, in a strange kind of way. I once thought we were friends, but looking back with the distance and knowledge of adulthood, I realized I had been just...convenient.

A thick vein popped in relief from his neck, and he looked about to roar like the beast he truly was. "I never thought you were. I just want to know: why?"

There were a million reasons why. Because I felt like it. Because I had nothing else now, now that I had lost my job. Because there was something bizarre and strange inside me that enjoyed the hunt. But more importantly, I had a promise to keep.

None of which were reasons I owed him.

So, I used the most potent weapon I had—guilt.

I went to close the door on him. "Go away, Lucas. You almost killed me last time. I lost my job because of what I did for you and your friends. I'm done with dragons, magic, fairy princesses, and immortal monsters. Leave me alone to my normal human life."

The attack worked better than I'd expected. My words were like water thrown onto his rage, melting it away to a stony expression. To my surprise, he let me close the door.

I locked the knob, the deadbolt, and braced my back against the door, as if that would stop him. If he were truly intent on pressing the issue, he could break it down with a sneeze.

I listened for footsteps and heard him walk away. Double-checking the security app on my phone revealed him leaving the building.

That was easier than I thought. Was it a residual effect of the armor?

I pulled up one of my robe's sleeves and looked at my smooth brown skin. For a moment, it remained the same. I concentrated, and my skin began to itch. Then black scales rippled forth.

I stared at them, shining, almost metallic.

Once, they had horrified me.

Now, for better or worse, they were a part of me, to be accepted like my brown skin, curly hair, and behind that was far rounder than I would have liked.

Months ago, I had agreed to help some old childhood friends. Like Lucas, they were also dragons—actually, they were his cousins—but unlike Lucas, they had made an attempt to keep in touch with me as we'd grown up. We liked and commented on each other's social media posts and had deep, if rare, chats over random things like the violent and tender nature of humanity and the best organic fertilizer for a container garden. I was still positive Daniel was using magic for his cherry tomatoes.

We had been captured by what I now understood to be literally an alien monster hell-bent on hunting and eating all magical creatures of Earth, of which there weren't many left. For some reason, the monster had placed mind-control bands on Lucas and me and forced us to try to kill one another.

The monster had also forced something else on me—a power that had given me odd, inhuman abilities.

Yet the witch Chloe, whom they had charged with my care after escaping from the Devourer's zoo, had said that I was free and clear of the monster's magic.

The scales along my arm flickered, responding to my thought of the Devourer with a visceral hate that at times felt more solid than the ground I stood on.

It was that hate that, strangely enough, made me feel safe about letting it live inside me.

From the images it had shown me, I knew this much: it was a symbiotic lifeform that had been a weapon of the dragons in their old world. It remembered being deployed against the Devourer when the dragons were fleeing to Earth. Its original bearer, a grizzly old bearded warrior whose favorite weapon was a massive axe bigger than my coffee table, had died when the Devourer destroyed the original dragon home world, but somehow, it had survived.

I couldn't get much else out of it. It otherwise expressed itself in feelings like rage and hunger.

It was the blood hunger that was most troubling.

Perhaps one day I would have to show someone what had happened to me.

But not right now. Not while Val was in trouble.

I dropped my arm, the sleeve falling and covering my scales.

Cursed I might be, but right now, I needed the monster's magic.

I had a serial killer to track down and a friend to save.

———

THE LINE to the club was out the door and wrapped around the corner. As I walked up in my four-inch golden heels, the music thumped in to the street, the rapper chanting between the beats of bass, "*Damn, girl. You got it, girl; you got it, girl.*"

It wasn't like I didn't have any experience hunting criminals. I had worked for the FBI after all. Not as an agent, but from behind screens, whiteboards, and closed doors. I was one of the many contract data analysts the bureau had employed until budget cuts killed the obscure department where I'd worked.

Of course, having Daniel turn in a resignation letter when I'd been in a traumatized coma hadn't helped the job situation either.

Lucas, covered with blood, screaming my name, as I swung a sword at his head.

I squeezed my eyes shut, slapping the side of my head as if I could knock the memory away.

The scales underneath my skin itched at the thought of the Devourer.

I took a deep breath, opened my eyes, and centered myself in the present.

Damn, girl. You got it, girl; you got it, girl.

I strutted up to Jamal, the bouncer at the front. He was a big brown bald monolith of a man, standing there, arms folded with a look designed to mean business.

"Hey," I said, with a smile. "Got some room in there for me?"

Jamal unhooked the velvet rope. I had helped his girlfriend

out of a sticky situation with some crooked cops not too long ago. "For you? Always."

I ignored the cold, jealous stares of the others in line as I entered through the doors into a universe of swirling flashing neon lights and a bass beat that reverberated in my core.

Damn, girl. You got it, girl; you got it, girl.

I wasn't much of a club goer, but I was here because this was the last place anyone had seen Val. We had taken different paths, but a long time ago, we were the only two brown girls in Oakwood Elementary. In kindergarten, she got in a fight with Tommy Warner, the mayor's son, after he'd broken my glasses on purpose and told me to go back to my own country.

I wished I could say that she had been my best friend from that day on.

But that's not the way things worked out.

Damn, girl. You got it, girl; you got it, girl.

Some guy with a backward baseball cap and his sneakers way too white made his way toward me, cup of beer sloshing in his hand. He planted himself in front of me and yelled. "Is your name Wi-Fi? Because I'm feeling a connection!"

I turned, and he put his hand on my left breast and squeezed. I glared at him in disbelief.

He shrugged with an unabashed grin. "You can't be wearing a dress like that and not expect to be touched."

I briefly checked the space behind him. All clear.

I smiled, put my hand in the middle of his chest, and shoved.

He went flying, crashing into empty barstools behind him as I put my best "whoops" face on, before disappearing into the crowd.

Shit, I was underestimating my strength.

I returned to dancing, shimmying and shaking my shoulders into the mess of people and letting the music come over me. I put my hands up.

Prey.

Once in a while, the armor spoke in my head, always when it was hungry, always when it sensed food nearby.

Something tingled in my head, indicating where the prey was. There was a momentary green shimmer around the man, a totally unremarkable guy with ash-blond hair. Average height, short hair, a black collared shirt, and he surveyed the crowd from behind a drink like any number of other people watchers.

I caught his gaze and smiled as I shimmied and turned.

That was something I had never understood about clubs— all the people who came to sit and drink and watch people dance without being part of the dance themselves.

Prey.

Damn, girl. You got it, girl; you got it, girl.

I danced my way through the crowd toward him. Once more, I made brief eye contact with him and smiled. And then I turned my back and ignored him for a few minutes.

Hunger erupted inside me, so empty, so dry, craving the taste of fresh warm blood.

My own horror blossomed alongside it, the human part of me that knew this feeling wasn't right, wasn't normal.

And just as quickly, the gaping maw of hunger was gone, as if it had severed the connection between us.

Then just the simple word again.

Prey.

When I caught the quarry's eye again, he gestured to the empty seat next to him.

I turned away and danced a little more, making sure to shake my ass at him and letting the lights play over my shimmering gold dress.

In a few minutes, I made my way to the bar and casually stood next to him. I ordered a drink, something expensive, and looked at him.

"Put her drink on my tab," he said, his stare glued to my exaggerated and exposed cleavage. If the neckline were any lower, I'd be showing nipple. "Those were some nice moves."

At least it wasn't another Wi-Fi pick-up line, though he got no points for originality. "Thanks."

He opened his jacket and handed me a card. "I run an agency of sorts. I have some prestigious clients who I think would be very interested in you."

He thought I was an escort. Perfect. "I'm not for sale."

"I wasn't implying that you were." Underneath the clashing club scents of smoke, pot, liquor, sweat, perfume, cologne, no wait –

Bleach.

Acid.

Just like the other serial killers I had found.

TEXTS WITH HUNTER & SOPHIE

ON HUNTER'S FAMILY TRADITIONS

Sophie: I love you, but stripping almost naked and singing songs in the middle of the night around a campfire to bring the baby good fortune isn't exactly my idea of a vacation.

Hunter: It's an ancient dragon tradition meant to bless the child. And it's not an ordinary campfire; it's the Fire of Life, lit by an elder dragon, burning sacred herbs to help you and the child relax.

Sophie: It's not pot is it? I'm pretty sure getting high while I'm pregnant isn't exactly healthy for the baby.

Hunter: No...At least I think not.

Sophie: You think?!

Hunter: I've never been to one of these things.

Sophie: That's not helpful.

Hunter: It will be fine. And then afterwards I'll bring you hot cocoa, from the fancy chocolatier in Manhattan that you like, my darling food snob.

Sophie: Watch how you talk to the MOTHER OF DRAGONS.

Hunter: 🐉 ?!?!?!?!SOPHIE!?!?!?!?

Sophie: Thats's what you get for calling me a food snob. 😋
   And I finally got you to use emojis!

Hunter: DRAGONS?!?! PLURAL?!

Sophie: Still singular. It just sounds so much more dramatic when it's plural 😘😘

***

If you liked that peek into their life, my newsletter has more snippet stories like this and exclusive awesomeness, like pictures of my actual writing desk (ok not so awesome, considering that there is a diaper (CLEAN) on the desk, but that's what I'm about.
   (I get REAL on my newsletter.)
   What are you waiting for?
   Click below to sign up!

https://www.karalockharte.com/dragonlovers1-signup/

Made in the USA
San Bernardino, CA
13 May 2020

71675778R00097